D1348446

One Stormy Night
MARILYN PAPPANO

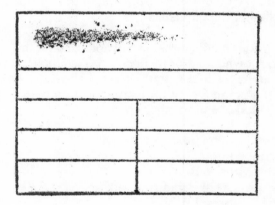

 MILLS & BOON®

Pure reading pleasure™

First published in Great Britain 2008
Large Print edition 2008
Harlequin Mills & Boon Limited,
Eton House, 18-24 Paradise Road,
Richmond, Surrey TW9 1SR

© Marilyn Pappano 2007

ISBN: 978 0 263 20144 4

Set in Times Roman 16½ on 19 pt.
34-1008-65956

Printed and bound in Great Britain
by Antony Rowe Ltd, Chippenham, Wiltshire

MARILYN PAPPANO

brings impeccable credentials to her career—a lifelong habit of gazing out of windows, not paying attention in class, daydreaming and spinning tales for her own entertainment. The sale of her first book brought great relief to her family, proving that she wasn't crazy but was, instead, creative. Since then, she's sold more than forty books to various publishers and even a film production company.

She writes in an office nestled among the oaks that surround her home. In winter she stays inside with her husband and their four dogs, and in summer she spends her free time mowing the yard, which never stops growing, and day-dreams about grass which never gets taller than two inches. You can write to her at PO Box 643, Sapulpa, OK 74067-0643, USA.

Prologue

The house creaked as the winds buffeted it. Jennifer Burton spared only a glance for the scene outside—night-dark sky, pouring rain, trees flailing wildly—before turning back to her task.

Hurricane Jan was just off the coast of Belmar, Mississippi, and everyone with any sense had already evacuated inland. Jennifer planned to join them just as soon as she found what she'd come to the house for. As chief of police, Taylor was far too busy to worry about what his wife was up to; he'd never dream that she'd returned to their house, a scant mile off the beach with Timmons Creek flooding through the backyard.

He would never dream she'd found the backbone to search for, much less run off with, evidence to use against him.

Something smashed into the house, vibrating through the boards and brick, making her jump as she opened the door into Taylor's study. The forbidden room—that was how she'd come to think of it in the three years they'd been married. The day they'd returned from their honeymoon and moved her belongings into the house, he had taken her to the closed door. *This is my room. You don't clean it. You don't look for anything inside it. You don't even cross the threshold. Understand?*

Her sister, Jessica, never would have allowed a man to ban her from entering a room inside her own home. She would have made a habit of going in just to spite him and she would have left traces that she'd been there.

Jessica never would have allowed much of what Taylor had done.

Encouraged by the thought of her sister, Jennifer stepped inside. The overhead lights flickered as the wind continued to batter the house. Phone service was already out and the roads were flooding—she'd had to take a detour to get there. Soon the storm would come ashore and damage or destroy everything in its path.

She hoped Taylor was in its path.

Her hand trembled on the flashlight she'd brought along just in case. She didn't know what she was looking for, but she knew in her bones that, whatever it was, Taylor was hiding it here. Financial records, perhaps; there was no way the city paid enough to account for even half of his extravagant lifestyle.

Maybe blackmail records. She'd heard whispers that the police department coerced and intimidated regular payments from most of the businesses in town.

Maybe…maybe… She didn't know, and the thunder of a tree crashing into the house next door reminded her that she had precious little time to waste. She would take everything she could—the contents of the file cabinet, the desk drawers, the closet on the far wall.

She packed quickly, first into boxes, then slid the boxes into black trash bags to protect them from the rain. As she filled each bag, she carried it down the back stairs, then ran back to start again. She worked without thinking about what she was doing or about how furious Taylor would be. What he might do to stop her. How much she had once loved him.

Until she opened the closet door and found herself at eye level with a shelf of DVDs. Every one of them was labeled, in Taylor's writing, with a date and a woman's name.

Or a girl's name.

She'd dropped several into her bag when she picked up the most recent, marked May of that year, along with the name Tiffani Dawn. Everyone in Belmar knew who Tiffani Dawn Rogers was. Pretty, blond, sixteen years old, grew up on the wrong side of town, wild and re-bellious, in trouble on a regular basis since she was ten…and now dead. She'd gone missing after attending the rowdiest of the high school graduation parties, and her body had been found three days later.

Two days *after* the date on the DVD.

Dear God.

Hand shaking badly, Jennifer carried the DVD to the entertainment system that filled one entire wall. The press of one button turned on the television; another powered up the DVD player. It took two tries to press the Open button, three failures in opening the jewel case.

She didn't want to see this. She'd accepted that Taylor wasn't the man she'd thought he was. He was sometimes cruel, always arrogant and, though she'd denied it to herself for two and a half years, corrupt. He misused his position as police chief and abused his authority. He was petty, his charm a camouflage for a mean spirit and an ugly soul.

But, please, God, surely he'd had nothing to do with Tiffani Dawn Rogers's murder.

Outside the wind howled, swaying the house fractionally. Still clutching the closed case, she went to the window to peer out, but darkness and churning rain blurred everything. She'd never been in a hurricane before. She was a California girl; earthquakes and mud slides were more her speed. She didn't know how much time she had to escape.

But she needed to see the DVD. She needed to know whether her husband was just a common criminal…or a murderer.

She was turning away when a flash of light caught her attention. It was a car half a block away, moving slowly in her direction. Who, besides her, was so late in evacuating?

The answer came when the vehicle—an SUV, not a car—eased to a stop at the end of her driveway. It was black and white and bore the seal of the Belmar Police Department. Heaven help her, it was Taylor, probably come to retrieve his own valuables, accompanied by the assistant chief.

Panicked, she stared at the DVD. If he caught her with it, he would be enraged. Darting across the room, she shoved the tray on the DVD player shut, then turned off the power. Downstairs the front door slammed. She stretched onto her toes and dropped the case behind the decorative molding on top of the entertainment center. Voices sounded at the stairs, one muffled, the other growing louder as it came nearer.

Grabbing the bag with the other DVDs, she raced out of the room and toward the back stairs. She reached the turn in the staircase just as Taylor's voice became audible and stopped, creeping from one step to the next.

"…take me a minute, then we can get the hell out of—"

His curse was loud and colorful. He must have discovered the door to his study open.

She was two steps from her goal—the kitchen, the gloom outside making the lights look brighter. They shone like spotlights on the two plastic bags there—would shine like a spotlight on her for the few seconds it would take her to dart out, then around the corner to the garage door.

One step…then Billy Starrett's voice rang out. "Hey, Burton, why are all these lights on? And why'd you leave the garbage sitting in the middle of the kitchen fl—" He stopped in the doorway, eyes widening when he saw her huddled there on the last step. His hand groped automatically for his pistol but found his yellow slicker instead. While he fumbled to get it open, she balled the open end of the bag around her fingers and ran, not to the garage door but to the back door.

His yell for Taylor was snatched away by the wind as she ran, head ducked against the driving rain, bag cradled tight to her chest. She ran to the end of the deck, scrambled down the steps and tore off across the lawn. Waterlogged grass grabbed at her shoes, slowing her steps, but she pushed on, into their neighbor's yard, sticking close to the solid shadows of the house as she headed toward the next yard.

She thought she heard Taylor scream her name, but that didn't slow her. Heart pounding, legs pumping, she ran mindlessly, her only destination *away*. When a powerful flashlight beam sliced through the dark, she ran harder, veering away from the houses and their obstacles, cutting across open lawn. The street was beyond the houses to her right—faster for her, but faster for Taylor, as well—and Timmons Creek ran to her left, flowing over its banks, its normally sluggish pace churning now.

A crack sounded nearby—a breaking limb or a gunshot?—and she dashed toward the trees that lined portions of the creek. She gave the bag a great heave into the brush but didn't slow even though her lungs were burning, her muscles quivering.

Just ahead her trail ran out. A six-foot-tall fence ran right down to the water's edge. She could run along it, which would take her to the street, or she could go into the water. She was a strong swimmer. She would take her chance with the creek.

She was only a few feet from the water's edge when something slammed into her from behind. Taylor. She would know his touch anywhere. She landed facedown, his weight suffocating her, half in the water, half out. Then the weight was gone. Kneeling astride her, he flipped her over, staring down at her with such rage that she hardly recognized him.

"You disloyal bitch!"

She struggled with him, bucking her hips, clawing at his hands, his arms, his face. They moved deeper into the water, the current tugging her one way, Taylor the other. She landed a few blows and took a few that made her vision go blurry.

And then suddenly the rushing water won, pulling her away. It lapped her face, eased her aches, and the upsurge blocked Taylor's shouts as he splashed after her. Falling to his knees, he disappeared under the water's surface, then struggled to his feet again and shouted a curse as she washed out of his reach.

For the first time since meeting him, she was free.

Chapter 1

By one o'clock on Tuesday morning, Belmar, Mississippi, was pretty much asleep. The stoplights on Main Street were turned to flashing yellow, the bars had had last call, and nothing remained open for business but the twenty-four-hour convenience stores and gas stations on the east and west ends of Main.

"This will never work," Jessica Randall murmured as she cruised down a deserted street, making mental notes of places Jen had already told her about—the grocery store, the hair salon, the bank, the church she had attended with

Taylor and, of course, the house she'd shared with him, as well as the police station. One place Jessica couldn't avoid—and one she would try to stay hell and gone away from.

"Of course it will." Jen's face smiled at her from the screen of the cell phone mounted on the dash. "We're identical, all the way down to the matching appendectomy scars, though I think mine is neater than yours. Besides, look at all the times we took each other's places growing up— and we never got caught."

"Me going out on a date for you is one thing," Jessica retorted. "Trying to fool your husband—"

"Estranged husband."

"—is totally different."

"Taylor knows I have a sister, but he doesn't know we're twins. He also knows that we've kind of lost touch since the wedding. You won't have any problem. Now, I've told you about the apartment, the house and the people. I have some things in a storage unit on Breakers Avenue. I don't think I would have hidden anything there, though. I mean, it's so obvious, and Taylor does tend to pick up on the obvious."

Jessica's mouth tightened. *Kind of lost touch?* For twenty-five years they'd been as close as two people could be, and it had taken less than a week for Taylor Burton to come between them. A stupid Caribbean cruise—that was where they'd met, where he'd charmed her into marrying him before the ship returned to Miami. And it wasn't even supposed to have been Jen on the cruise. Jessica had made the reservations for herself, but when business had called her to Hong Kong, she'd persuaded Jen to go in her place.

It was fate, Jen had all but cooed when she'd finally resurfaced to tell Jessica—by phone, no less—that she'd gotten married, and without her twin.

Shouldn't fate be good for more than three lousy years? Shouldn't it take longer than thirty-four months for Prince Charming to turn into a toad? And a criminal-scum toad at that.

"Jess? Are you listening to me?"

"Yeah, I'm listening. You haven't remembered

anything else? What I'm looking for? Whether it's bigger than a bread box?"

"Not a thing." Jen sounded regretful. "I wish I knew, I wish I could retrieve it myself. But…"

She couldn't. And because she couldn't, the solution was obvious: Jessica would. She was the older—even if only by three minutes—the bolder and the braver.

She turned onto the other main street, Ocean Street, then moved into the right lane. All her driving and she hadn't seen a single police officer out on patrol, though there had been three cars parked in the reserved lot behind the station. It looked as if when the town called it quits for the day so did the police department. Did the criminals also call a nighttime moratorium? Or in Belmar were the police and the criminals one and the same?

If their chief was anything to judge by, the answer to that was a resounding yes.

The Sand Dollar Apartments had once been the Sand Dollar Motel, until competition from the newer motels on the east and west sides of town had put it out of business. The building had been renovated into apartments, small, plain, nothing fancy. Jen's was on the back side of the building, facing a narrow parking lot and a park complete with playground, soccer fields and noisy children on most nice days.

What had once been twelve units on the ground floor was now six one-bedroom apartments, with four two-bedroom apartments on the second floor, and every third parking space had been turned into a tiny patch of yard with spindly trees in some, flowers in others. She parked in front of #8 and cut off the engine. She'd seen Taylor's three-hundred-thousand-dollar house, and yet Jen had spent her last two months in Belmar living in a converted thirty-dollar-a-night motel. How intolerable had the house—or, rather, the marriage—gotten?

Jessica hadn't brought much with her—her laptop, a small bag with toiletries. She would wear Jen's clothes, her perfumes, her jewelry. She'd already had her hair cut to match Jen's short, sleek style and had indulged in fake fingernails in Jen's usual pale pink to disguise her own shorter nails.

She was there and she was ready to begin the charade. As soon as she got a good night's sleep.

Streetlamps at the corners of the parking lot drew halos of insects that buzzed ceaselessly. The air was muggy, both temperature and humidity higher than she was accustomed to. Dim lights burned in a few units, but there was no sign of life. No televisions blaring, no parties going on, no traffic on the street out front.

She gathered her belongings plus a grocery bag. *Bring snacks,* Jen had warned, and she'd stopped at one of the convenience stores for that and water. Singling the key from the others on the ring, she fumbled it into the lock, then swung open the door.

Musty. Unbearably hot. Stale. The apartment had been locked up since the hurricane, the air-conditioning off. Wishing she'd bought a can of air freshener or scented candles, Jessica flipped the light switch next to the door, but nothing happened.

The weak illumination from the parking lot

lights showed a pale shadow about the right height for a lamp shade in the near corner. Jessica felt her way toward it, found a lamp, turned the knob—and again nothing happened.

Okay, Jen liked balance. If there was a lamp at one end of the couch, there would be another at the other end. Jessica eased her way along the edge of the couch, making it halfway before stubbing her toe on something. Glass toppled with a crash, then rolled off the edge of what seemed to be a coffee table and landed on the carpet with a thud.

Damn, she should have brought a flashlight—and worn tennis shoes. Her big toe was throbbing, and she'd probably chipped the polish, after subjecting herself to a pedicure at Jen's insistence.

Finally she reached the end of the sofa, finding another table and another lamp that didn't work. Great.

Surely the kitchen had an overhead light. She headed that way, bumping her hip hard into a side table on the way, knocking over something more substantial. Swearing softly, she extended

both arms in front of her in the hopes of prevent-
ing any more damage to herself as well as Jen's
furnishings. Her hands connected with the
smooth surface of a countertop, swept back to
the wall, then up. She'd just found a couple of
light switches when something hard pressed
against the base of her skull.

"Police. Who are you and what are you doing
here?"

The voice was male, deep, menacing, and it
made swallowing all but impossible over the
lump that had suddenly appeared in Jessica's
throat. *Showtime,* Jen whispered inside her head,
but when she opened her mouth, nothing came
out but a squeak.

She was the older, the bolder and the braver,
she reminded herself.

And he's got a gun!

As the protest formed, the pressure on the back
of her head eased and she felt the space between
them widening. He was backing off—the better
to shoot her without getting blood and brains on
himself, the hysteric in her warned.

"Hands in the air, then turn slowly."

Her left hand was already in the air, she realized. She drew the right back from the light switch, raised it, as well, then turned slowly, as he'd instructed.

With the dim light at his back, all she saw was shadows, but that was intimidating enough. He was at least six foot two, with shoulders broad enough to fill the doorway. *Hulk* was the first word that came to mind. He had a gun and he worked for Taylor the scum.

And *she* was pretending to be Taylor's wife.

She drew a breath, straightened her shoulders and said, "You protect and serve even in the middle of the night. I'll be sure to tell my husband how diligent you are."

For a moment the air in the room seemed to vibrate. Just as quickly, the moment passed, and there was a rustle of movement, the click of a switch, then light flooded the dining area. The enemy stared at her and she stared back.

She'd been close with *hulk* but definitely one letter off. This guy was a *hunk*. Tall, broad, great chest, narrow hips, long legs, muscular and golden brown all over. She could see that because he wasn't wearing anything but boxers that rode low on the aforementioned hips. He didn't need a weapon to make a woman swoon; just one good look at him in his current state of undress would do the trick nicely.

Tall, dark and hot. That meant he was Mitch Lassiter, and she'd been right on one point. He *was* the enemy.

His expression was impossible to read. Shock? Dismay? Suspicion? Doubt? He could be feeling anything or nothing, and she'd never know, thanks to the utter blankness on his features.

Feeling as if she were taking a chance she shouldn't, she lowered her arms and crossed them over her middle instead. "I suppose you have a reason for harassing me inside my own apartment."

He moved as if to put the gun away, but there was no place to put it. He settled for laying it on the glass dining table a foot to his left. "Other than the fact that you're supposed to be dead, no."

"Dead." Holding her arms out to her sides, she turned in a slow circle. "I assure you I'm very much alive, Officer Lassiter." Jen had never encouraged familiarity with any of Taylor's employees, though she'd had little choice with Billy Starrett, the assistant chief. He and his wife, Starla, had constituted the bulk of their socializing.

Starla Starrett. Can you imagine? I'd've kept my maiden name.

His gaze narrowed as he studied her. His hair was dark brown and so were his eyes. If eyes were the windows to the soul, this man's soul was hard. "Where have you been?"

"I wound up in a hospital, then a shelter. My sister came back to the U.S. after the hurricane, and I spent some time with her."

"And you never thought to call your husband?"

The same husband who'd punched his wife and held her head underwater? It would be all Jessica could do to see him without smacking him hard. "Estranged husband," she pointed out.

"Does he know you're back?"

"I'm sure he will once you scurry home and call him like a good little police officer."

His gaze narrowed even more, and a muscle clenched in his beard-stubbled jaw. *I don't like Mitch,* Jen had said. Though she hadn't mentioned it, the feeling was evidently mutual.

"He's been worried about you."

"So worried that he tells people I'm dead?"

"You were seen leaving the apartment with your car loaded. Your car was found a few days after the storm where it had washed off the road near Timmons Bridge, with everything still in it. You didn't call anyone."

"I called my sister."

He looked as if he wanted to say something to that, but she didn't give him a chance. "It's late, Officer Lassiter. I'm tired. And I'm sure you're just dying to get to a phone so you can report in to Taylor. Please close the door on your way out."

A moment passed before he finally picked up his pistol, then turned to the door. His muscles were taut—heavens, he had a great back and backside, too—and his movements graceful as he stalked across the room, walked outside and left the door standing open.

Another moment passed before Jessica was able to move. Lacking his grace and trembling more than a little, she hurried over, closed and locked the door, then put on the security chain for good measure. Not that it would stop someone determined to come in, but it gave her a small measure of extra comfort.

As she righted the items she'd knocked over in the dark—a vase on the coffee table, a statue on the side table—she admitted that she was probably going to need whatever comfort she could get in the days to come.

Jennifer Burton was alive, well and back in Belmar.

As Mitch dialed Taylor's number, he wondered how his boss would take the news. *He* was sure as hell disappointed by part of it. Not that he wished Jennifer dead, of course. But he had thought that if she'd escaped the hurricane alive, she would have had the sense to not come back to Belmar. After all, it was Taylor's own private kingdom, where she was his own private property. He wasn't the sort to let a woman go unless he wanted her gone, and there had seemed something not quite right about her car at the Timmons Bridge. As if the scene had been staged.

About half of the town had presumed she was dead, and Taylor had been among them. If it had been his wife, Mitch wouldn't have given up hope until there was none left to hold on to. He would have personally searched every shelter, walked every inch of the county looking for a clue and gone to every hospital, clinic and doctor's office within a three-state area. He would have printed flyers and offered rewards.

Not Taylor. And yet all through their separation he'd sworn he loved her and wanted her back.

On the third ring, Taylor picked up, his voice groggy, his words slurred. "Thish better be 'mergency."

"Depends on your point of view, I guess."

"Hey, Bubba." That was followed by a loud yawn. "What's up?"

That was what Taylor had called him ever since they were kids, when Mitch had come to Belmar to live with his grandmother just down the road from the Burtons. They'd been nine years old and adversarial in the beginning. After Mitch—three inches shorter and fifteen pounds lighter—had whipped Taylor's ass, they'd become good friends and remained so, though not as close as they once were. After college, Taylor had returned to Belmar, while Mitch had taken a job in Atlanta. They'd kept in touch, though, and eventually Mitch had found himself back in town again.

Mitch wasn't sure about the etiquette for breaking the news to someone that his loved one wasn't dead, so he said it bluntly. "Jennifer came home tonight."

There was utter silence on the line. Mitch would give a lot if he could see Taylor's expression. Most people weren't as good at hiding their feelings as Mitch was. Just a flicker could tell him a lot.

"So she's alive." Taylor sounded wide-awake now and his voice was quiet. Thoughtful. "Is she all right? How does she look?"

"Fine." Mitch smiled without humor. She looked so damn much better than fine that it was laughable. Jennifer Burton was a beautiful woman. Blond hair, blue eyes, a cute little nose, a mouth made for kissing. She was five-six, maybe five-seven, slender but with enough curves to make a man grateful. Whatever part of the female anatomy a man preferred, she fulfilled every fantasy and then some. She was sexy as hell in a wholesome girl-next-door type of way.

The *married* girl next door.

"Did she say anything about where she's been?"

Mitch repeated what Jennifer had told him.

"Her sister, huh?" Taylor said, then the silence returned. He'd never met Jennifer's older sister and had never wanted to. Jennifer's life was with him, in Belmar, he'd proclaimed. Everything and everyone in her past should stay there.

As if you could just shut out family because someone else told you to. Mitch hadn't even been raised in the same state as his brothers, but he still had regular contact with them.

"She's alone?"

"Apparently."

But the rustle of background noise on the phone, followed by a murmur—a sleepy female murmur—indicated that Taylor wasn't. When he'd mentioned the marriage in a call to Mitch six months after the fact, he'd joked about how long he would be able to stay faithful to his wedding vows.

Jeez, his wife had presumably died only three weeks ago, and he had another woman in his bed.

Scowling, Mitch rubbed the throbbing between his eyes. He and Taylor had been friends for more than twenty years, but there was a lot he didn't like about the man. Though there was a lot he didn't like about life in general, and Jennifer Burton's return was probably going to add a few things to that list.

"Thanks for calling, Bubba."

"Are you going to see her?" Mitch asked, aware it was none of his business.

"I've waited three weeks. Another night won't matter. I'll see you tomorrow."

Slowly Mitch hung up. In the first week after

the hurricane, Taylor had been the personifica-
tion of the grieving husband, especially after
Billy Starrett had located her car. Even his worst
enemies—about half the town—had felt sorry
for him. Now, fourteen short days later, his dear,
beloved wife had suddenly rejoined the living,
and he couldn't be bothered to leave his girlfriend in bed to go see her.

Mitch moved his gun to the nightstand on the
right side of the bed, then went to the kitchen to
get a bottle of water from the refrigerator. He
stood at a counter identical to the one where he'd
first spotted Jennifer and stared disinterestedly.
The room was the standard motel room turned
into a living room, a dining area and a tiny
kitchen. The former connecting door led into the
bedroom and bathroom. The cheap motel shag
had been replaced by a decent-quality carpet,
and the walls had been painted bland off-white.
It was boring but clean, everything worked and
it wasn't even in the same universe as the worst
place he'd ever lived.

Though it well might be the worst place Jennifer

Burton had ever lived. It was sure as hell a huge step down from Taylor's house over on Beachcomber Drive. She was a tad materialistic. Though she'd worn jeans and a sweater tonight, he would bet they were hundred-bucks-plus jeans, and the sweater was probably silk or cashmere. She was expensive, Taylor had often said with pride, because he could afford to keep her.

He made sixty-two thousand dollars a year and paid his officers less than a third of that. Yet he lived in a four-thousand-square-foot house in the best part of town, drove a Hummer that was less than a year old, took regular ski vacations to Colorado, an anniversary cruise every summer and three-times-a-year gambling trips to Las Vegas. His wife dressed in designer clothes and had enough jewels to stock a small shop. His fishing boat must have set him back forty grand, and her recently junked Beemer had had less than five hundred miles on it.

Something wasn't right in Belmar, and Mitch wanted in on it. Taylor had promised him the time was coming, but he was growing tired of waiting. This apartment might be a hell of a lot better than the worst place he'd ever lived, but it was also a hell of a lot worse than the best. He wanted to move on.

Water gone, he returned to the bedroom. He'd rented furniture when he'd moved in—bed, nightstands, dresser and a desk, plain and functional. The sheets were white cotton, the bedspread light brown. The only items of a personal nature in the room were his pistol, his wristwatch and his laptop.

There was nothing personal he wanted anyone in Belmar to see.

A thump came from next door, drawing his gaze to the connecting door that had survived the renovations. Jennifer's bedroom was on the opposite side of that door. Her bathroom backed up to his, and sometimes, before the hurricane, he'd heard her shower running while he'd been in his. Sometimes he'd fantasized...but not often. She was a married woman. Married to his boss. His oldest friend.

That meant something to him even if it didn't seem to matter to Taylor.

He slid between the sheets, shut off the light and, with a weary sigh, closed his eyes.

The rumble of a finely tuned engine woke Jessica Wednesday morning. She blinked, needing a moment to remember where she was, then rolled over to glare at the drape-covered window. To her, cars were transportation, nothing more, nothing less, but whoever owned this one—likely male—was probably extraordinarily proud of the noise it made.

Probably next-door male, she reflected. Mitch Lassiter.

The prospect of seeing him wasn't what drew her out of bed and across the room. She just wanted to see if it was daylight yet—such grumbling should be illegal between the hours of sunset and sunrise.

She parted the curtains an inch or so and peered through the gap. The car, parked a few spaces away, was an old Mustang, midnight-blue and a convertible. That was the best description she could offer. The owner *was* next-door male, and he was fiddling with something under the hood.

He wore clothes this morning—khaki trousers, khaki shirt with dark green epaulets, green tie, black shoes and black gun belt, complete with gun. Black and lethal was the best description of *that* she could offer. His hair was a shade short of shaggy, and his jaw was clean-shaven. He looked sinfully handsome. Dangerous.

He straightened, wiped his hands on a rag, then closed the hood. Abruptly he looked over his right shoulder. She dropped the curtain, then took a few steps back for good measure. Her face flushed, as if she'd been caught spying on him. Granted, she had, but the odds that he knew that were minimal. He couldn't possibly have seen her, couldn't even know she was there.

Unless he noticed the slight sway of the curtain as it settled.

Shivering in the morning chill, she grabbed her robe, adjusted the thermostat, then went into the bathroom. When she emerged thirty minutes later, showered, shampooed, powdered and lotioned, the Mustang's rumble was gone.

Older, bolder and braver, she scoffed. Officer Lassiter could intimidate her with nothing more than his presence—and he wasn't even the real danger. According to Jen, Taylor was the boss in both his law-abiding and lawbreaking pastimes. Everyone else, including Mitch, just did what they were told.

Not that he struck her as much of a follower.

In the kitchen, she rooted through the grocery bag for something to calm her stomach. The choices were chips, popcorn, cookies, cupcakes and a half-dozen of her favorite candy bars—her idea of "staples." She settled on popcorn, washed down with a bottle of diet pop, then sat down at the glass table.

She was going to have to face Taylor today. Given her choice, she wouldn't see him at all, but the odds that he would let her waltz into town after having been missing for three weeks without seeing her were somewhere between slim and none. Belmar was a small town. The first time she walked out that door, the gossip would start to fly. People would be watching

Taylor for a reaction, and he wouldn't let them down. *She* wouldn't let them down.

Every weekday, according to Jen, Taylor had breakfast at the diner across the street from the police station. Joining him were a select few of his officers—his *corrupt* officers. She thought they did it as a show of force, reminding the other customers that they stood together, that they were in charge and there was little anyone could do about it.

A restaurant seemed as good a place as any for Jessica to meet her brother-in-law—correction: her pretend estranged husband. Public. Safe.

She dressed in a skirt and blouse from the closet. The labels were pricey, the fabric and workmanship excellent, but puh-leeze…the skirt was a floral print that covered her knees and the blouse had a ruffle around the modest V-neck. Granted, it was a wide, kind of flirty ruffle that draped nicely, but she hadn't voluntarily worn ruffles since she was two, when they'd covered the butt of her diaper-padded sunsuit.

"Oh, Jen," she said on a sigh as she studied

herself in the mirror. "What did he do to your fashion sense?"

She applied makeup with a very light hand— *Taylor likes the natural look*—and sprayed on Jen's top-dollar perfume, then grabbed her purse and left the apartment. The clothes made her feel more like an impostor than ever.

The day was sunny, and already the combination of heat and humidity was oppressive. She drove the half-dozen blocks downtown and found a parking space in the middle of the block. Flipping down the visor, she checked her face in the mirror, then cut her gaze to the cell phone dangling from her purse strap. "I could use a little encouragement," she murmured, but the phone remained silent.

With a breath for courage, she got out of the car, walked to the restaurant and stepped inside. The dining room was full, but locating Taylor was easy; he and his officers occupied the largest table and made the most noise. At least until they became aware of her.

The place literally fell silent as Taylor stood.

He was exactly as Jen had described him—
blond, blue-eyed, tanned, with a cleft in his chin
and a crook in his nose. He had a nice body,
though not as nice as Officer Mitch, a devil whispered in Jessica's head. He looked strong,
capable, authoritative, the kind of man who had
always appealed to Jen's fragile-woman sen-
sibilities. How sad that she'd fallen so hard for
his outside that by the time she'd learned what
he was like inside it was too late.

When he smiled, it would probably stop
women in their tracks, but he wasn't smiling
now. He simply stared, showing no surprise, no
emotion at all. Of course, he'd had about seven
hours to get used to the idea that she was back.
Since her oh-so-nosy neighbor had blabbed.

And speaking of the devil, sitting to Taylor's
left was Mitch himself. Unlike everyone else in
the place, whose attention was ping-ponging
back and forth between her and Taylor, his gaze
was fixed on his boss, watching him as if he
might see straight through Taylor's head and into
his thoughts.

Curious.

Now what should she do? Approach Taylor? Snub him? Join him at his table and see if he would send everyone else away? Take a table of her own and wait for him to come to her?

He came to her before she could decide, stopping too close, but she held her ground. "Jennifer. Nice of you to come back." His expression was bland, his words very soft, but he was very angry. She didn't need to know him to recognize that.

"Taylor." Her fingers itched to punch him just once...okay, as many times as she could before his goons pulled her off. She wanted to hurt him, to make him pay for what he'd done to Jen.

That's why you're here. To make him pay. Never forget that.

"Were you planning to let me know you were back?"

"You knew. Our friendly neighborhood cop told you, did he? But even if he hadn't, I would have called you today. Tomorrow. Sometime."

He smiled thinly and lowered his voice to a

chilling whisper. "It wasn't nice of you to let us think you were dead."

"Sorry about that. I was more concerned with recovering from my injuries than with what people back here were thinking."

His jaw tightened, his gaze narrowing. "You took something that belongs to me. A lot of things. I want them back."

When she'd walked inside the diner, it had been only a few degrees cooler than outside. Suddenly she was so cold that she thought she might never get warm again.

Whatever Jen's evidence was, as long as he'd thought it had disappeared with her, it was only a minor worry. Virtually any type of evidence— paper, computer CD, flash drive, photographs— would have likely been destroyed in the storm.

But if Jen survived, so did the threat to him. And that made him an even bigger threat to Jessica.

"Sorry," she said again. "I don't have a clue what you're talking about. Now, if you'll excuse me, I'd like to get some breakfast." With a polite nod—and a private sigh of relief—she moved around him, walked to the nearest empty booth and sat down.

Taylor stood motionless for a moment, staring where she'd stood. Abruptly he came out of it and actually snapped his fingers at his men. Everyone jumped to his feet except Mitch, who rose but slowly.

When he came even with Taylor, Taylor stopped him, murmured something, then followed the rest of the officers out the door. Jaw taut, Mitch returned to his chair, settled in and picked up his coffee. He didn't look like a happy camper.

Hands trembling and heart pounding double time with delayed reaction, Jessica ordered the morning's special, then downed a glass of water. It was foul but still left a better taste in her mouth than the encounter with Taylor had.

Jen had warned her that coming here would be dangerous, that Taylor would kill her if he got the chance. Their brief encounter had left Jessica with no doubts about that. Taylor Burton was one very angry man. His career, his freedom and his life were at stake. He wouldn't lose a moment's sleep if he killed his supposed wife to protect himself.

He might want her dead but not until he recovered whatever Jen had taken.

A group of diners left and another came in, a posse of old men wearing faded work clothes and gimme caps. They headed automatically toward the large table but stopped when they saw it was occupied. One of them flagged down the nearest waitress. "It's after nine o'clock," he grumbled. "That's been our table for twenty years. They get to use it before nine. Not after."

The waitress looked at Mitch—who was ignoring them and showing no intention of leaving—shrugged helplessly and headed for the kitchen with an armful of dishes.

While the men complained among themselves none too softly, Jessica slid to her feet and walked to the table. "I take it you're the designated…babysitter? Spy?"

Mitch studied his coffee cup for a time before meeting her gaze with open hostility. It was his only response.

"I figured. Why don't you keep tabs on me from over there—" she gestured to her booth "—and let these gentlemen have their table." Without waiting for an answer, she returned to her seat and began eating the breakfast that had been delivered in her absence.

He slowly stood, dropped what looked like a ten on the table, then started her way. No one else from his group had paid, she realized. They'd left their plates mostly clean and walked out without so much as a quarter for a tip. Free meals and good service—two of the benefits of being a cop, Taylor the scum used to say.

Dear God, Jen had told her so much that she felt as if she knew the man.

A moment later, the air took on a shimmer of tension, then Mitch sat down across from her. She chewed a bite of ham, took a nibble of buttered toast, then sprinkled salt and hot sauce over her hash browns. "This is some job you have, Officer Lassiter. Surveilling the boss's wife."

"Estranged wife," he corrected.

She allowed a small smile. Once Hurricane

Jan had blown through, Hurricane Jen would have swept Taylor right into divorce court—and, hopefully, criminal court. He would have soon been her ex-husband and grateful to see the last of her. But she hadn't gotten the chance.

"Would you like my schedule for the day?" she asked helpfully. "When I leave here, I'm going to the bank. That should take about ten minutes. Then I need to stop by the post office—five minutes or so, depending on the line. Then the grocery store. I cleaned out the refrigerator before the hurricane, so I need to restock. Though I wouldn't be surprised if you already knew that."

She raised her gaze to his face, watching the muscles in his jaw tighten. "Truthfully, I wouldn't be surprised if you people had been in my apartment on numerous occasions in the past three weeks. Searching for signs that I'd planned to evacuate, looking for clues, for evidence, for…oh, whatever might catch Taylor's fancy."

His hard gaze turned even harder as she murmured, "No, I wouldn't be surprised at all."

Chapter 2

Mitch's coffee had long since gone cold, so he quit pretending interest in it. He was pissed off at being assigned babysitting tasks, pissed even more by Jennifer's condescending recital of her morning plans and most of all by her implication that he'd done something wrong in checking out her apartment.

"No response, huh?" She looked as if she expected nothing more. "What is it Taylor says? 'Admit nothing. Deny everything.'"

Yeah, he'd gone to her apartment, gotten the key from the manager, let himself in and searched the place, but it had all been part of a missing-person investigation. Taylor had met him there, and they'd looked through her closet, her drawers, her cabinets. Taylor had made a list of the obvious things missing—some clothing, two suitcases, makeup and photographs—and then he'd asked Mitch to leave him. He'd wanted time alone in the apartment.

And Mitch had left. Separated or not, Jennifer was still Taylor's wife. He'd feared the worst from the beginning. He'd been emotional. Though not too emotional this morning upon seeing her for the first time since he'd thought she'd died.

Mitch studied her, making no effort to hide it. She looked pretty damn good in a married-minivan-soccer-mom sort of way, but he liked her better in last night's tight jeans and snug top. There was something entirely too demure about the over-the-knee skirt and the prissy top.

Seeing that she *was* married, estranged or not, he should find "demure" good. He shouldn't be thinking that she needed to show more leg, more skin in general, or that she should only wear clothes that hugged her curves.

He shouldn't be thinking about her as a woman at all.

"You don't have much to say about your work, do you?" Jennifer asked. "Let's try something else. Where do you come from? You're obviously not from around here."

"'Obviously'?" he echoed cynically. "I lived in Belmar from the time I was nine until I went away to college. You'd think Taylor would have mentioned that."

Her cheeks tinged a faint pink that quickly faded. "Taylor tells people what he wants them to know when he wants them to know it. All he ever said was, 'Bubba and I go back a long way.' With Taylor, that can mean a month or twenty years."

"Twenty-four years, to be exact."

That was an accurate description of Taylor, though. Hadn't he talked to Mitch a half-dozen times after his wedding before he'd mentioned it? Even then, he'd been stingy with information.

Jennifer Randall. From California. No one you'd know. Over the next couple years he'd offered little more: they'd met on a cruise; she'd taught grade school in California; she had an older sister; she wasn't much of a cook.

Taylor liked holding his cards close.

"Does your family still live here?" she asked.

"They never did. I lived with my grandmother. She died while I was in college."

"I'm sorry." She sounded as if she meant it. "So where does your family live?"

"My mother's in Colorado. My brothers live in Georgia."

"And your father?"

"Died when I was nine." The child-support checks had stopped coming, and his mother had sent him to her mother. It sounded an awful lot like abandonment but hadn't felt that way. He'd liked his grandmother and she'd liked him. Living with her had been easy.

"So you came here, but your brothers didn't. Were you a problem child?" She asked it with a wry smile that he couldn't read. Because she was stating the obvious or because she didn't really believe he'd been bad enough to send away?

He smiled thinly. "I was an illegitimate child. When the old man died, his sons—my half brothers—continued to live with their mother. My mother sent me here."

Except for the monthly checks, his father had never acknowledged him. His brothers and their mother hadn't known he existed until Sara had come across the record of those checks when settling his estate. She had invited Mitch for regular visits, given him time with his brothers and treated him more like a son than his own mother had. She had even asked him to live with them, but he'd chosen to stay with his grandmother. Even so, he considered Sara more family than his mother.

"I'm sorry," Jennifer said again, and he realized he'd just told her more about himself than even Taylor knew. Not good.

"Why did you come back?"

He turned the question on her. "Why did you? Half the town was betting that the storm would

be the shove you needed to leave Belmar and
Taylor for good."

"And what did you think?"

"I didn't. Frankly it didn't matter to me
either way." A lie. He'd been curious. Had
thought it one hell of a waste if she was dead.
Had hoped if she was alive, she was smart
enough to stay gone. Had thought she deserved
better than Taylor.

"You didn't answer," he reminded her. "Why
did you come back?"

She poked her fork at the last bits of hash
browns on the plate, then laid it down and pushed
both away. "I had unfinished business here."

Her only business in Belmar, unfinished or otherwise, was with Taylor. Settling matters between
them? Divorce? Reconciliation? Revenge?

He figured Taylor's interests lay more in line
with revenge. People didn't go without his say-so.
If an officer decided to leave the department,
Taylor fired him before he got the chance. Back
in college, when word had gotten out that he was
going to be cut from the football team, he'd quit

first. He wouldn't have liked that Jennifer had left him. He'd want to win her back, if for no other reason than so he could turn around and leave *her.*

Hey, no one had ever accused Taylor of maturity.

"You should have gone back to California with your sister," Mitch said flatly.

She glanced at the check, then left a generous tip on the table before meeting his gaze again, hers straight, blue, steady. "Is that a threat, Officer Lassiter?"

He kept his gaze just as straight and steady. "Why, ma'am, I'm an officer of the law. I don't make threats."

Her snort showed just what she thought of that. His brief experience with the Belmar Police Department—two months and counting—supported her opinion.

There had to be *some* advantage to a job that paid what this one did, Billy Starrett often repeated.

He followed her to the counter, where she paid her ticket, then out the door. Her car was parked down the street; his was around the corner. She walked a few feet away, then turned back.

"Remember—bank, post office, grocery store." Then, with a smirk, she walked off.

Damn Taylor for giving him this order. Mitch had better things to do, things that actually fell under his job description. Using department assets to find out what the chief's wife was up to wasn't exactly appropriate. But, when compared to all the other inappropriate things going on within the department, this one didn't begin to matter.

He climbed into his unit, switched the AC to high, then fastened his seat belt. He'd spent more years in a patrol car than he wanted to count at the moment. With a shotgun secured to the dash, a heavy-duty flashlight in the passenger seat, the radio, the computer and the extra handcuffs tossed onto the console, he felt comfortable here, more than anywhere else in Belmar.

There were three banks in town, but he didn't have to guess which one Jennifer was going to. She tapped the horn as she drove past, just to make sure he didn't miss her. She was entirely too accommodating about being watched to be up to anything. It promised to be a long, boring morning.

She went inside the bank and spent eleven minutes and got in and out of the post office, with a handful of mail, in six. Her next stop was the grocery store nearest the apartments. He parked behind her car and across the aisle and watched as she went in.

Ten minutes passed. Fifteen. The engine was running and so was the AC, but the temperature inside the car was steadily rising. Southern Mississippi was always hot and humid in September but seemed even more so that morning. Maybe it was Hurricane Leo, idling out in the gulf, deciding which way to blow. Maybe it was this assignment, being used as a babysitter— spy—on city time, that was making him hot. Or, hell, maybe it was the whole damn job.

Restless and needing to do something that felt productive, he called in the tag on her car to the dispatcher, Megan, who ran it and notified him, predictably, that it came back to a rental company. He asked her to call the company and find out who had rented it. She said something to someone there in the office before replying affirmatively, and he recognized her voice from last night's call to Taylor.

So Megan was sleeping with the chief. Great for job security...until she did something to tick him off or he found someone he wanted more. Like his wife?

It took a few minutes for Megan to call back with the info, and she did so on his cell phone. "The car was rented by Jessica Randall, who lives in Los Angeles. You think she's related to Taylor's wife?"

You think?

"I know she's back. What do you think she wants? Where has she been? What has she been doing?" Dispatcher and department gossip—Megan's unofficial title.

"You'll have to ask Taylor. Thanks for the info." Mitch hung up as a vision of blond hair, golden skin and frilly clothing came out of the grocery store, only one small bag in hand, and started his way. He rolled down the window as she neared. "Why is your car rented in your sister's name? Why didn't you do it?"

Dark glasses covered her eyes, hiding their expression. He wore dark shades, too, but she wouldn't be able to read any more if she were looking straight into his eyes.

"What do you need to rent a car, Officer?"

"Driver's license and credit card."

"And what did you find inside my washed-away car besides two suitcases, some jewelry, cosmetics and a few mementos?"

Her purse, with her driver's license and credit cards.

"Jess rented it for me before she left. She knows I'm good for it. And speaking of good…" She held up the shopping bag a moment before depositing it in his lap. "I realized this is going to take me a while, so I thought you might need to cool off."

One part of his anatomy was quickly turning ice-cold until he lifted the bag and looked inside. It held a bottle of chilled water and an ice cream sandwich.

For the first time in a long time, he was taken by surprise. Under the circumstances, she was the last person he would have expected a thoughtful gesture from. "I—thank you."

She flashed a smile. "I'll be out soon as I can."

She strolled back into the store, long legs taking long steps, hips swaying. When had he ever seen Jennifer Burton *stroll?* When had he ever watched her do *anything?*

God, he needed a break. A date. A woman.

Any woman who could make him forget all about his boss's wife.

Jessica loaded more groceries and cleaning supplies than she could possibly use into the trunk of the rental, climbed behind the wheel and glanced at Mitch before backing out. He'd finally shut off the engine and rolled down the windows and he looked hot. Sweat dotted his forehead and likely dampened his shirt as well as his hair. Damp was a good look on him. Wet would probably make her steam.

The cell phone beeped and she punched the speaker button. "It's about time you called."

"How's it going?" Jen asked, her voice ethereal and disembodied through the small speaker.

"I met Taylor this morning and he's a jerk. What a loser."

"Oh, I thought he was amazing when we met. He was so handsome and charming and adorable." She sighed. "Of course, I didn't know then what I know now."

"I also met your next-door neighbor."

"Mrs. Foster? She's kind of a pain—oh, you mean Mitch Lassiter."

Who was also kind of a pain, Jessica thought with another glance in the rearview mirror.

"You know you can't trust him."

"As if I need you to tell me that." Bad cop or not, Taylor's friend or not, Mitch Lassiter was the sort of man any smart woman watched out for. Handsome enough to make Taylor look like a toad, sexy enough, too, but lacking in charm, and *adorable* simply wasn't in the vocabulary that applied to him. He was dark. Hard. Dangerous.

And, according to Jen, if not already on Taylor's payroll in more ways than one, soon to be. No matter how handsome and sexy, a corrupt cop…she just couldn't stomach that.

"Do you have a plan?"

Jessica laughed. "Yeah. Getting the groceries

out of this heat and into the kitchen while Officer Mitch sears to a crisp in the parking lot."

"Taylor has him watching you."

"Bingo." Jessica turned into the Sand Dollar, slowed to about five miles per hour and drove to the rear of the building.

"You can't search for anything with him watching you."

"I can start inside the apartment, though I'm pretty sure he and Taylor have already checked it out." He'd refused to confirm or deny it over breakfast, but it stood to reason. Jen had been missing; they were cops. Knowing that Taylor had been inside the apartment Jessica was temporarily calling home, touching things that she was touching, looking at the clothes she was wearing, was creepy. Knowing that Mitch had created an inappropriate sensation all its own.

"Listen, I'm home and Officer Mitch is pulling in beside me. Give me a call later." She disconnected and climbed out before he'd had a chance to shut off the motor. She opened the apartment door first, the metal hot enough to burn, then carried two handfuls of bags inside to the kitchen counter.

When she turned, he was blocking her way, sunglasses off and the rest of the bags in his strong grip. She swallowed hard, her chest tight, backing up until the refrigerator stopped her and giving him access to the countertop.

She'd been right about the sweat dampening his hair and his shirt—right that hot and sweaty was a good look for him. Of course, the *way* he'd gotten hot and sweaty could make it an even better look, she thought, then chided herself. He was the enemy, remember? It was a given that everyone who worked for Taylor was on his side. *Trust no one,* Jen had intoned, and she hadn't laughed when Jessica had. She'd been deadly serious.

If Jessica didn't keep her guard up, she could end up seriously dead.

He set down the bags, then retreated to the dining table, and suddenly she could breathe again. "Th-thank you." For carrying in the bags? Or for giving her space? She didn't know. Didn't care.

He shrugged as if both his actions and her words meant nothing.

"Tell your boss I'm planning to spend the rest of the day at home, so you'll be free to do your real job."

Something flashed through his eyes—annoyance, perhaps. With her for being smug? Or with Taylor for assigning him to such a mundane task? "I don't think he's likely to take your word for it."

"Well, if he makes you stay, at least you can stay inside. You won't die of heat exhaustion. I keep it cool."

Where had *that* come from? The last thing she needed was a cop hanging around while she looked for evidence that would incriminate his boss and quite likely him—and the last thing she wanted was more time in his company.

He gave her a narrow look, assessing, as if he might discover her ulterior motive for the invitation if he looked hard enough. Abruptly, though, he turned away. "The heat's not going to kill me."

It felt as if the statement was unfinished—*but something else might*—but that was all he said.

With a muttered, "Later," he left the apartment, and this time he closed the door behind him. A moment later, she heard the distant thud of her trunk closing. She walked to the window and peeked through the crack in the drapes and saw him leaning against a tree barely tall enough to support his weight in the tiny lawn next to her car, his cell phone to his ear, no doubt calling Taylor.

Now there was a conversation she would love to eavesdrop on.

She was still standing there, minutes after he'd ended his call, when another police car rolled around the corner. It stopped behind her car, and Mitch walked over to talk for a moment to the man behind the wheel. Then he got into his own car, backed out and drove away, and the new guy took his space, right next to her rental.

The guy was probably older than he looked—he looked about eighteen—and wore mirrored sunglasses above a scraggly mustache. He'd been with Taylor in the diner that morning, which meant he wasn't to be trusted. What was the world coming to, some TV show character had once asked, when you couldn't even trust the police to be honest?

Amen to that.

She double locked the door, closed that little gap in the drapes, then returned to the kitchen. Except for a few frozen dinners, most of her food purchases had been of the junk-food variety. She and Jen had been blessed with a good metabolism that allowed them to eat that way without worrying about their weight. There at the end, Jen had been spitefully pleased that Taylor tended to get fat if he didn't exercise religiously and stay away from sweets.

What about Mitch? Those muscles hadn't appeared out of thin air, but did he work out because he needed to or simply liked to?

"What does it matter?" Jessica asked aloud, loading her voice with every ounce of frustration. "He's one of the bad guys, remember? Just this morning you were criticizing Jen for falling for a pretty face, yet you're on the verge of doing the same thing."

Letting out a low, annoyed growl, she turned, hands on her hips, to survey the living room. It was time to start searching. She knew Taylor's men had already searched the apartment and had, presumably, found nothing. That meant one of three things: Jen had hidden it extraordinarily well, in plain sight or someplace else.

She had her work cut out for her.

Wishing she could open the drapes and let in the sun without the kid cop being able to see, she turned on every light in the room—and discovered the reason the lamps at either end of the sofa hadn't worked the night before: they were unplugged from the wall. Jen had always unplugged things like hair dryers and can openers before leaving the house, believing they were fire hazards. With a faint smile, Jessica stuck the plugs back into the outlets and the lights immediately came on.

After plugging in the television, she tuned it to a music channel, then started her search. It was a good thing the apartment was so small. Because she intended to do a very thorough job.

* * *

"Is he in?" Mitch asked as he passed Megan. Without interrupting her broadcast, she nodded in the direction of Taylor's office.

He wound between desks, passed the interrogation room and paused long enough for a sharp rap at the door before opening it and inviting himself inside.

Taylor leaned back in his chair, hands folded over his stomach. "Well?"

After moving a stack of files from the lone chair that fronted the desk, Mitch sat down and made his report—every stop Jennifer had made, why and for how long. The only parts he left out were the ice cream and his helping carry in her groceries. There wasn't any reason not to tell him about either. Mitch just didn't want to.

That done, he said, "As long as she knows she's being watched, she won't do anything interesting, so I'm going out on patrol."

"That's fine for now. I've got Jimmy Ray over there. Sitting in the car watching the apartment just might be what he does best."

What Jimmy Ray did best, Mitch thought, was threaten people. He looked so young, so harmless, that no one suspected he was mean as the devil until it was too late. Not that he would ever do anything without Taylor's order. Tough as he was, he knew Taylor was tougher.

"But I want you to watch her at night and on weekends."

Mitch stared. He'd like to believe Taylor wasn't serious, but he'd lost whatever illusions he'd had about his old friend weeks ago. "I'm not being paid—"

"You will be." Taylor's voice was as level as his expression. "You keep an eye on Jennifer on your time off and you'll find a nice raise in your next paycheck."

Mitch settled back, crossing one ankle over the other knee. "Using department resources and department money to investigate your wife... And I suppose if I find anything that could be useful, say, in a divorce, that would probably earn me a nice departmental bonus, wouldn't it?"

"I'm not worried about a divorce," Taylor said

dismissively. "You have a problem with making some extra cash?"

Mitch considered it, then lifted one shoulder in a shrug. "Depends on how much cash we're talking."

"It'll be enough. Trust me. Just keep an eye on her. She's a beautiful woman. It won't be hard. Okay?"

Again Mitch waited a beat before agreeing. "Okay."

He was at the door before Taylor softly added, "Bubba? Just an eye. You lay a hand on her...I'd hate to consider the consequences, what with you and me going back so far."

Mitch opened the door, then glanced back. "I don't fool around with married women." He looked pointedly in Megan's direction. "There's something about those vows..."

Taylor didn't even look uncomfortable, much less guilty.

As Mitch returned to his car, he wondered what had happened to Taylor over the years. His parents were still together after some forty years;

they spent summers in Alaska and winters in South Florida and they'd always seemed happy. His father had been a lawyer, his mother a stay-at-home mom, and in their retirement they did regular volunteer work with children's charities in both states.

Through high school and college he and Mitch had had far more in common than not. They'd shared an apartment, taken the same classes, even had the same plans of going into law enforcement. Taylor had returned home to Belmar, though, while Mitch had gone to Atlanta for big-city police work within a few hours' drive of his brothers.

Somewhere along the way, though, Taylor had changed. He'd become more controlling, more self-centered, less honest. He'd always been a little on the wild side and more than a little full of himself, but within limits. Back then he'd given a damn about something besides himself and power and money. Mitch felt as if he hardly knew him anymore.

Felt as if he hardly knew himself.

One thing about working law enforcement in a

town where most of the police department was corrupt—there wasn't much other crime to investigate. Since coming to Belmar, Mitch's days were mostly spent writing traffic citations, with the occasional teenage vandalism, burglary or drug bust. People on the chief's good side got special attention when they were the victim of a crime and a blind eye when they went speeding through town. That had been the toughest problem Mitch had faced since coming to town—keeping straight who was on the chief's good side.

Until Jennifer had returned.

"Don't lay a hand on her," he scoffed. As if he needed to be told. He'd kicked Taylor's ass twenty-four years ago and could easily do so again in a fair fight. Not that Taylor fought fair. He used his badge, his authority and his department to intimidate and frighten. He was rarely seen without one or more of his officers. He believed in making a show of force and in letting others do his dirty work.

That was the man Mitch had called friend for twenty-four years.

He drove to the north edge of town, where an abandoned gas station stood across the street from a big, relatively new truck stop. What the station owner hadn't hauled away, thieves had, and vandals had broken the rest. The only thing that still worked on the premises was the pay phone, only because it was around the corner, on the side of the building where weeds grew tall. He backed his car into the weeds, beaten down because it was one of his few routines. With the highway coming into town and the speed limit dropping from fifty-five to thirty in the space of a few hundred yards, it was a good spot to work radar.

Leaving the coolness of his car, he dropped a few coins into the pay phone, then dialed his brother's cell phone.

"Calloway." Loud music played in the background, raunchy and punctuated by louder, rowdier male voices.

"Jeez, it's not even noon and you're already in a strip joint?"

"It's noon somewhere," Rick said. "Besides, I

get paid to be here. I'm tending bar. You still in Mississippi?"

"Where else?"

"How does the small time compare to Atlanta?"

"I'm more likely to die of boredom here than there."

"Yeah. Some guy gets bored and shoots you to liven up his day."

Mitch had heard the joke before, but he still grinned. Wouldn't that be something—after eleven years on the streets in Atlanta, to get killed in the line of duty in a nowhere place like Belmar. "The only person liable to shoot me down here is my boss, and that's only if I get too friendly with his wife."

"She worth getting shot over?"

He didn't even need to close his eyes to summon up an image of Jennifer in last night's second-skin jeans and sweater. When he'd first come up behind her in the dark, he'd smelled her fragrance, subtle, just enough to tease a man, and felt the heat radiating from her before he'd taken a step back for safety. His, not hers.

"She could be, if she wasn't married," he replied, earning a grunt from Rick. Funny thing about Mitch and the Calloway boys—having a father who wouldn't keep it in his pants had given the meaning of *fidelity* one hell of an impact. He hadn't been kidding when he'd told Taylor there was something about those marriage vows.

"Other than the boss being a tad possessive about his wife, how's it going down there?"

"Okay. He offered me a raise if I keep an eye on her."

"She's worth getting shot for, and he's not sticking close enough to keep track of her himself?"

"They're separated. Remember? She went missing in the hurricane, he thought she was dead. She's not and she's back, and he wants to know everything she does."

"Why doesn't he hire a private investigator who specializes in divorce cases?"

"When he can let the city pay me to watch her?" Mitch scowled as a car sped past on the way into town. The city manager's teenage son

was behind the wheel and he was at least twenty
miles over the limit. Lucky for the brat that his
father was on Taylor's good side.

"Funny thing," he went on. "Taylor's not
worried about a divorce."

Rick was silent for a moment, considering
that. Mitch thought about it, too. Taylor didn't
have a prenup—he'd mentioned that before. He
had a lot of assets, most of which couldn't have
been funded by his salary. It was hard to imagine
that he could possibly have anything on Jennifer
that would make her walk away from the
marriage with nothing. Taylor, guilty of something worthy of blackmail? Sure. No doubt.
Jennifer? No way.

"Maybe he plans to win her back," Rick suggested.

"Maybe." Or maybe he had other plans for her.
But this was neither the time nor the place to
discuss that in depth. Anywhere else in the
country, phone calls, especially from pay
phones, were relatively safe as far as privacy.
But Belmar wasn't anywhere else.

"Well, there are worse people that could be watching her."

"And worse people to have to watch." But damned if he could think of a single one. If there was a woman in town with the ability to screw with his concentration the way Jennifer had, he hadn't met her yet.

"When you get that raise, why don't you come up here and take us out for a weekend on the town?"

"Isn't that a night on the town?" Mitch asked drily.

Rick snorted. "A night's not even enough to get started. Mom said to tell you she misses your ugly mug and she wants to know when you're coming to visit."

"I'll call her when I get a chance."

"Yeah, just be careful what you say."

Mitch rolled his eyes. What was it with people stating the obvious to him? Did he look that dumb? "Jeez, thanks for the advice. I probably would have blurted out everything, going all the way back to that pretty blonde who lived across the street from you guys and taught me every-thing a fifteen-year-old boy could bear to know when I spent the summer there."

Rick gave a low whistle. "Kayla Conrad. Son, she taught *all* of us all we could bear to know. Man, I haven't thought of her in years. Tell you what—you stay there in Mississippi and I'll go home for a visit. I'll give Mom—and Kayla—your best."

"You do that." Though if anyone could take his mind off the crappy state of his life at the moment, it might be Kayla.

Jennifer could make him forget. For a while. Then they would put their clothes back on and come back to their senses, and life would be even crappier because he would have broken one of the few rules he lived by. Taylor would find out and Mitch would suffer the consequences—and with people like Jimmy Ray on Taylor's payroll, *suffer* was definitely the right word.

Scowling, he said goodbye to his brother, then returned to the car and switched on the radar unit. He was frustrated and annoyed, a prime combination for writing traffic tickets.

Taylor might be paying him illegally from the city's coffers. But at least Mitch would know he'd done his best to increase those coffers first.

Chapter 3

A minute shy of six o'clock, Jessica ran out of steam.

She'd taken every CD and DVD out of its case, checking for original labels, and flipped through the pages of every book. She'd looked behind every picture and painting and underneath every shelf and drawer. She'd unzipped the sofa and chair cushions and tipped the furniture upside down, searched for loose tiles in the kitchen and bathroom and crawled the perimeter of the apartment checking for places where the carpet might have been pulled up. She'd heaved the mattress and the springs off the bed, dragged the frame from the wall so she could see behind it and taken every single item from every drawer, cabinet and the closet.

In the process, she'd discovered that Jen had been an amazing housekeeper, gotten hot and dirty and found nothing. Now, after a shower, she was calling it quits for the evening and heading out to dinner. Snacks could only take a woman so far.

"Going somewhere?"

She started as she locked the door but thought she did a decent job of hiding it. Letting her key ring dangle from one finger, she turned to find Mitch kicked back in a folding lounge chair underneath the scrawny oak. He wore denim shorts, faded and soft, and a Belmar High School basketball jersey that looked about twenty years out of date.

He looked incredibly hot—and she didn't mean his temperature.

"To dinner." She moved to the edge of the grass, wishing she were barefoot like him and could curl her toes into the cool green growth.

There she could see a beer can on the ground next to the chair and a book open in his lap. She recognized it as the one she'd read on her last flight from Hong Kong—a thriller about a vulnerable woman taking on police corruption.

She chose to ignore the book. "Drinking on duty. Why am I not surprised?"

"Not much surprises you, does it?"

She shrugged.

He picked up the can, drained the beer, then crumpled the aluminum. "I'm not on duty."

"Uh-huh. After following me around town this morning, you just happen to be sitting outside my door now by coincidence?"

"No coincidence. I sit out here most nights. I've been doing it since I moved in here— which, by the way, was *before* you moved in. Look." He rolled to his feet with more grace than any man should show and lifted the chair easily in one hand. "There are places worn in the grass from the legs."

The three faint lines showing where the chair had spent many hours were impossible to deny.

So was the foolish feeling that curled through her. *You could have told me that, Jen.*

Of course, there was no response from her sister.

"I'm going to that little barbecue place out on the east side of town," she said. "In case you lose sight of my car on the way."

Tilting his head, he studied her a moment before saying, "I told you, I'm not working. But if you want my company for dinner, all you have to do is say so."

She blinked at the remark, thoroughly unexpected. She wanted his company like she wanted a hole in her head. He was Taylor's buddy. The enemy. Not to be trusted.

But someone was going to be watching her. Better him than the creepy kid who'd hung around part of the morning and all afternoon. Even with the drapes drawn, she'd known the kid was there, had *felt* his presence.

"I assume this restaurant requires shoes and a real shirt."

"This is a real shirt," he protested.

She looked at the jersey. Truthfully, it was perfectly adequate, particularly in a beach town. But it showed a lot of smooth brown skin and muscle and sinew and all that other sexy physical stuff. She would be lucky to taste her dinner, and the same could probably be said for any other female diners in the restaurant. Since she was a firm believer that barbecue, especially Southern barbecue, required all of a diner's attention, she repeated, "Shoes and a real shirt."

Scowling, he carried the chair, book and can into his apartment, then returned two minutes later wearing a pair of disreputable running shoes without socks and a black T-shirt with the same denim shorts.

He still looked hot.

"We'll take my car," he announced.

Jennifer was used to Taylor making unilateral decisions. Jessica was used to making decisions for herself. "What if I want to drive?"

He looked from the Mustang to the rental and his lip curled in a sneer. "Yeah, right."

He was right. The temperature had dropped by fifteen degrees, but it was still a warm evening, with a nice breeze blowing in off the gulf. Who in their right mind would choose the standard rental-car sedan over a vintage Mustang convertible?

He headed toward the Mustang. It took her a moment to get her feet moving. Somewhere deep inside her brain she was sure both her sister and her conscience were telling her what a bad idea this was, but some other part of her she didn't even want to put a name to—the risk taker? the woman? the fool?—was sticking her fingers in her metaphorical ears and babbling to block them out. It was just a short ride to the restaurant. Dinner. A short ride back. They would actually be alone ten, fifteen minutes tops. No big deal.

The Mustang's leather seats were midnight-blue to match the exterior and still held the sun's heat. She settled into the passenger seat, squirming a little, and fastened the seat belt. As Mitch started the engine, she dug a pair of sunglasses from her purse, put them on, then glanced at him. "Is it supposed to vibrate like that or is something wrong?"

He gave her a look she'd seen before—the

condescending car guy pitying the uninformed noncar guy. "Nothing's wrong."

She wasn't about to admit it, but she kind of liked the quiet rumble that all but growled "power." She wondered how fast the car would go, how a hundred and twenty miles an hour would feel through her hair, whether he ever kicked it up and let it out. She liked the sun on her face, as well, and the feeling of openness and freedom. Maybe she would buy a convertible when she returned to Los Angeles...and choke on all that L.A. smog.

She was enjoying the ride enough that it took her a few moments to realize that they weren't headed east. She looked around, not recognizing the road he'd turned on, then jerked her gaze to him. "This isn't the way to the barbecue place."

"This is the way to my favorite barbecue place. It's better."

"But—" She swallowed hard, the skin on her neck prickling. The street they were on was apparently part of Belmar's poorer side of town.

While the downtown area held a certain old-fashioned charm and the highways leading into town were the stereotypical gas station/motel/fast-food strips, these blocks were just shabby. The businesses were run-down, built of cinder blocks or occupying converted old houses. The houses themselves were dilapidated, as well, and interspersed with the businesses, as if the concept of residential versus commercial hadn't made it to this neighborhood.

"Relax," Mitch said, then suddenly grinned wolfishly. "Trust me."

Yeah, right.

As buildings of any sort came farther and fewer between and her heart rate started edging into double time, he slowed and turned into a gravel-and-shell parking lot. Down Home Q had once been someone's home, with a steeply pitched tin roof and a wraparound porch. The roof was streaked red with rust, the siding aged to silver. If paint had ever coated the boards, there wasn't so much as a flake remaining. Dark screens covered the open windows, and music and voices drifted out, along with tantalizing aromas.

Mitch parked at the end of a ragged row of cars, and they climbed the steps to the porch, where a screen door opened into the foyer, now a waiting area. The floors were wide planks of wood, the finish worn over the years, and faded cabbage-rose paper covered the walls. A wide doorway to the left opened into one dining room, a similar door on the right led to another and a hallway straight ahead went into the kitchen.

For a moment Jessica again debated the wisdom of coming here with him. Hadn't she been stared at enough for one day? Then she took another look around. Down Home Q wasn't Taylor's sort of restaurant. Jen had given her pretty much the minutiae of his likes and dislikes, and this place hadn't been mentioned at all. So far, none of the diners, plentiful in both rooms, had given them more than a disinterested glance.

A young girl came from the kitchen, her broad grin doubly bright against her ebony skin. She was about twelve, tall and gangly, waiting to grow into both her body and her beauty. "Hey, you. Daddy's been wonderin' where you are. Pick a table, and I'll see if I can find someone willin' to wait on you."

"Aw, Shandra, you know your older sisters all fight to wait on me," Mitch said with a wink.

She pretended to be unimpressed, but the corner of her mouth was twitching with a smile. "Yeah, you bein' such a good tipper and all."

"We'll be outside."

Mitch Lassiter, Taylor's thug, teasing with a twelve-year-old girl. *Not much surprises you,* he'd told Jessica earlier, but that did.

She followed him back out the door and around the corner. There were two tables on the porch there, each with four chairs, and a box fan was braced on the railing and turned to low.

"To discourage the bugs," he said as he sat down.

She sat opposite him, out of reach of the sun's setting rays. The chairs were metal, mismatched and painted different shades. The table was metal, too, sporting layer upon layer of paint.

The most recent was lavender; chipped places showed flamingo-pink underneath. In the center were salt and pepper shakers, a bottle of pepper sauce, ketchup, a roll of paper towels and packets of moist towelettes.

She folded her hands on the tabletop, moved them to her lap, then rested her arms on the chair arms. "The food smells good."

"It's the best you'll find in town."

She thought of the familiarity with which the girl had greeted him and the mention of her father. "You're a regular?"

"I'm here two or three times a week. Willis's barbecue is the best part of coming back to Belmar."

"I hope that says more about my cooking than it does the town." A tall, round man, presumably Willis, set two glasses and a pitcher of iced tea in front of them, then offered a menu to Jessica. "I'm Willis Pickering."

"Jennifer Burton."

His gaze cut to Mitch only for an instant, then he shook the hand she offered. "I know what

Mitch wants—once he finds something he likes, he doesn't change—but I'll give you a minute to look over the menu."

"That's all right." She set the menu aside. "I'll have what he's having."

"Two megaplatters coming up."

After he left, Mitch remarked, "Maybe you should have looked at the menu."

"I'm sure I'll like whatever I get. I'm easy to please."

He practically choked on his tea at that, tightening the muscles in her jaw. Jen had always been as easygoing as they came. She'd never asked for much out of life—a job she liked, good friends and family, someone to love. That big house, the new BMW, the expensive gems and fussy clothes—those hadn't been her choices. She would have been happy living in a trailer park wearing hand-me-downs as long as she loved her husband and he loved her back.

"Have you known Willis long?"

"Since middle school. We played football together."

"So he knows Taylor."

"Everyone in the county knows Taylor."

"And he doesn't like him."

Mitch shrugged.

"Most people in the county don't like Taylor," she said, mimicking his tone and his shrug.

That had been Jen's first clue that something wasn't quite right. From the beginning it had been clear that a lot of the people Taylor was sworn to serve and protect didn't think too highly of him—or of her for marrying him. There had been subtle digs, discomfort, sometimes outright hostility. It had bewildered her—she'd always gotten along well with everyone—but she'd written it off as an occupational hazard. Police chiefs made enemies.

Especially, she'd learned nearly three years later, corrupt ones.

Jessica pushed that subject to the back of her mind. "So Willis is about your age and he has multiple teenage daughters. Did he get an early start or are you the late bloomer here?"

Mitch shifted to prop his feet on the chair

between them. "His wife had their first girl about three weeks after graduation and had another every year after until Shandra was born. She's number four."

"And you haven't even got number one yet." Not that he struck her as a particularly paternal man. She would have to see past his sexy-as-sin exterior to put him in the role of doting father—and she was having trouble with that. Enough trouble to be a concern...later.

"Nope, no kids. I did have one marriage, though. It started out great but ended when we realized we had nothing in common anymore."

"How long did that take?"

"Four years to find out. Another to do anything about it." His brow furrowed as he frowned at her. "You're pretty good at getting me to volunteer information I don't normally share."

She coaxed a faint smile and shrugged again. "I used to teach third grade. My students always found me easy to talk to."

"You're comparing me to a third-grader?"

His mildly insulted tone strengthened her

smile. "I think most men have quite a lot in common with third-graders. And second-graders. And kindergartners."

"So why aren't you teaching here?"

Jen had wanted to teach. She'd wanted to do *anything* besides sit home alone all day or socialize with Starla Starrett and the few others on Taylor's approved-friends list. But Taylor had refused. How would it look if his wife was working instead of home where she belonged?

Because she didn't like the answer to the question, Jessica ignored it, returning instead to a comment Mitch had made earlier. "So you played football. And basketball. Were you any good?"

"Good enough to get a football scholarship to Ole Miss. I played two years, had surgery on my knee, decided I didn't want to spend the rest of my life limping around and quit."

"I don't like football. Or basketball. Or baseball, golf, fishing, tennis, track..."

"Don't be shy," he said drily. "For years I lived football and basketball. I'm a die-hard Braves fan. And the first thing my brothers and I do when I go for a visit is head out on the river to fish a few hours."

"Your half brothers."

Mitch took another drink of tea, brewed strong and sweet enough to put a diabetic in a coma, and wondered why she stressed the "half" part. Did she have half or stepsiblings that she didn't like to give the same acknowledgment as her real sister?

In their family, Sara had discouraged the use of *half*. It was all or nothing, in her opinion. He and her sons were brothers or they weren't. And since there was no denying that they shared the same father, they had the "all."

"Yeah. My brothers."

"What do they do besides fish?"

"Rick has a habit of changing jobs. Right now he's tending bar. Robbie's a lawyer and Russ is in construction." Deciding it was time to take control of the conversation, he asked, "What does your sister do?"

"Jess?" She blinked for a moment as if considering what to say. "She works for a company that acts as a liaison to American companies wanting to set up shop in Asia. She speaks Mandarin and travels a lot and lives a much more exciting life than I do. She's older than I am. Much more sophisticated. Prettier, too." Pink colored her cheeks to go with her self-deprecating smile.

"I find that hard to believe," Mitch murmured as Willis's wife rounded the corner balancing plates in both arms.

Jennifer's blush deepened.

LaRae efficiently deposited plates on the table. "Ribs. Chicken. Polish sausage. Pulled pork. Bologna. Corn on the cob. Potato salad. Slaw. Fried okra. And Texas toast. Can I get you anything?"

Jennifer was staring at the table filled with food, her eyes wide. "A doggie bag...or four or five?"

LaRae laughed. "You haven't eaten here with him, have you?" she asked with a nod in his direction. "The two of you will do it justice. When you're done, just make sure the fingers you lick are your own." She said the last with a lascivious grin, then sashayed away.

Jennifer transferred that awed look to him.

"You eat like this two or three times a week and haven't dropped dead yet?"

"Do I look dead?" He damn well didn't feel it. Especially in one particular area.

They sat in silence for a time, concentrating on their food. Jennifer had made a surprising dent in her dinner before pushing the plate away and fastidiously cleaning her fingers with the wet-wipes. "Oh, my gosh. At least if I die, I'll die a happy woman."

"That's all it takes to make you happy?" His gaze narrowed on her. "Maybe you're too easy to please." Though if he had advance notice of his last night on earth, Down Home Q might figure in. But so would other things. Time to talk to his brothers and Sara. One last sunset at the beach. One last tumble with a beautiful woman—or at least one last kiss.

The sun had set, and the noise from the woods that backed the restaurant was increasing—something croaking, something singing, something cooing. He wiped his hands, then slumped more comfortably in the chair. He'd spent a lot of evenings on this porch, long before it had become a restaurant, and he'd swear this same table had been there then. Having dinner there eighteen years later with Taylor's wife had never remotely crossed his mind back then. Neither had working for Taylor. Knowing he was dirty. Sharing in the benefits of his corruption himself.

Jennifer shifted in her chair, the squeak drawing his gaze her way. She wore another skirt, this one white with thin blue stripes and hanging halfway to her ankles, showing just a bit of golden skin between it and clunky sandals. Her blouse matched the blue stripes, the fabric too heavy to even hint at the curves it concealed except where a belt cinched it at her waist. The outfit was matronly enough to offend Sara, who was more than old enough to be Jennifer's mother and dressed as though she'd raised three, and sometimes four, boys pretty much alone.

And none of that changed the fact that Jennifer was damned pretty. There was sort of a glow around her, warm and innocent and sexual, too.

Or maybe, he thought with a scowl, it was just the light shining through the window at her back.

"Where did you live before you came here?"

He took the time to lean forward, refill his glass from the pitcher and offer her a refill, then sat back again, cupping his palms to the sweaty cold glass. "Atlanta." The truth if a person didn't get too picky. He *had* lived in Atlanta. It just hadn't been the last place before Belmar.

"Were you a cop there?"

He nodded. Again the truth, and no secret. Taylor had let everyone know he'd hired a big-city police officer. He'd thought it had somehow boosted his own prestige.

"And you gave up your job there and living in Georgia, near your family, to come back here and be a cop in Belmar. The pay can't be as good. The opportunities for career advancement certainly can't be as good. And the benefits probably aren't as good—at least the legal ones."

Heat warmed the back of his neck. "Is there a question in there?"

She rested her arms on the tabletop and her gaze

connected with his. "A good cop should be able to figure it out. Why? Were you not very good? Did you give up the job in Atlanta or lose it? Did Taylor offer you something Atlanta couldn't?"

"I was a very good cop." He didn't expect her to overlook the fact that he'd ignored the other questions, and she didn't disappointment him.

"Did you quit? Were you forced out? Were you fired?"

The heat was spreading to his ears, but it was dark enough by then that he doubted she could see it. "Ask Taylor."

A sarcastic smile curved her lips. "I try not to ask Taylor anything these days. I don't exactly trust his answers."

"And you trust mine?" It was a simple question. The logical response for him to make. He didn't care if or how she answered it. He *didn't*.

Still, his muscles grew a little tighter with each second before she finally shrugged. "More than his."

The answer was more satisfying than it should have been, and he immediately tried to make it less so. Trusting him more than Taylor wasn't exactly a glowing endorsement. Anyone who knew Taylor trusted practically anyone else more than him. She still thought Mitch's integrity was doubtful—her questions made that clear. She just thought he might be the better of a bad bunch. Also not a ringing endorsement.

If he'd counted right, she'd asked eight or nine questions of him—more than enough. More than he usually allowed anyone who wasn't family. Deliberately he turned the conversation back to her. "Are you planning to divorce Taylor?"

The shadows thrown by the lights inside made it impossible to read her expression, but he suspected it had turned thoughtful. She sat silent a long time, toying with her glass, before finally smiling faintly. "It's late. I think it's time to go home."

Home. A little word with so many meanings. It could be a place or, he'd been lucky enough to find out twice in his life, people. Intimate—as in the place they shared for a few hours, a few nights—or individualistic. Her home. His home. Different places. Alone.

He considered protesting—it was too early; he wasn't ready—but she pushed her chair back, stood, then neatly slid the chair under the table. Regretfully he followed her to the front porch and the screen door.

Shandra met them there with the check and a brown paper bag. When Jennifer started to reach into her purse, he ignored her and traded Shandra cash for the bag. "Tell your mama to keep the change."

Her smile was slow and mischievous. "What change?" she asked before walking away with a sashay that was a pretty good imitation of LaRae's.

"She's going to break hearts someday," Jennifer remarked as they descended the steps to the parking lot.

"Speaking from experience?"

She was smiling when she stopped beside the Mustang. It deepened when he opened the door for her. "I'm flattered you might think so, but the only heart I've ever broken is my own." Smoothly she gestured. "What's in the bag?"

"Cobbler." Enough to share, though he never

had before. He settled it in the back floorboard, then slid behind the wheel and started the engine. "Is it really late?" It wasn't even eight-thirty. Though he got up for work most mornings at five-thirty, he wouldn't think about bed until at least ten o'clock.

"No."

Instead of turning left out of the parking lot and going back the way they came, he went right. Five miles and a series of turns later, they were on the interstate, headed east and accelerating. Traffic was light and stayed out of their way. By the time they'd gone a couple miles, they were traveling a hundred miles an hour, the wind rushing, the countryside racing past in a blur.

A glance at Jennifer showed that she looked way too serene for a woman speeding with her hair on fire. Her eyes were practically closed, and the corners of her mouth were turned up just a little. The breeze molded her blouse to her breasts, but her hair was too short to do little more than rustle.

He saw the trooper too late to matter, not that

he was concerned. About once a week he took the car out on the interstate and opened it up, and about once a week he passed one trooper or another like a bat out of hell. They always gave chase, and as soon as they recognized the car as his, they backed off.

The siren made Jennifer open her eyes and twist in the seat to look behind them. He felt her gaze on him even as he took his foot from the accelerator and the car began to slow. After a minute or two, the siren stopped, then the trooper came alongside and shook a finger in mock warning before slowing and turning onto the median.

Mitch was grinning when he became aware that the emotion coming off Jennifer had changed—grown stiffer, tauter. Something was clearly annoying her. As he settled in at the speed limit, he impatiently asked, "What?"

"How many tickets have you gotten out of because you're a cop?"

"A few. Hey, you don't own a car like this and not run it once in a while."

"Anyone else, he would have written a ticket."

"That's not true. I know him."

"My point. If he didn't know you, he would have stopped you."

"*My* point is that he wouldn't have written a lot of people, whether he knew them or not. That includes you. He has a thing for pretty blondes."

She wasn't flattered. "You paid for breakfast this morning and for dinner tonight. Why?"

The question left him feeling as if he'd missed part of the conversation. "I pay for every meal I eat out. Walking a ticket is illegal."

"Taylor does it all the time. I've never seen him pay a restaurant tab in Belmar. You were the only one in that bunch this morning who did."

"Yeah, so? Restaurants give cops free food all the time, and they do it everywhere, not just in Belmar. It's not a big deal. Just one of the perks of the job."

"It shouldn't be." She folded her arms across her chest. "Besides, there's a difference in the restaurants giving and the cops taking. Do you expect me to believe that the owner of that diner *wants* to give free meals to the whole police department every day? Or does he do it because you expect it? Because he's too intimidated not to?"

Abruptly Mitch swerved into the right lane, then took the next exit. He drove across the bridge, then got back on the interstate westbound. "*I* don't expect a damn thing. That's been going on a hell of a lot longer than I've been in Belmar."

"So that makes it all right? You don't see anything wrong with it? You don't feel obligated to do something about it?"

His answer came out gritted with clenched teeth. "I don't take free food. I don't intimidate people into giving me things. But, yeah, I do take advantage of the fact that I'm a cop to get out of speeding tickets once in a while. Big deal. Don't tell me you've never flirted your way out of a ticket, that you've never batted those blue eyes and smiled that pretty smile and said, 'Oh, please, I won't do it again if you could just let me slide this one time'?"

"Actually, I've never been stopped by a cop."

"Never? Are they blind where you come from? I've known cops who'd stop a pretty woman just to get her phone number—" Too late he broke off. That wasn't the sort of thing she wanted to hear just then. It made her scowl. Fingers clenching the wheel, he went on. "Considering how much you've benefited from the perks of Taylor's job, your disapproval comes off more than a little hypocritical."

"I haven't—" She broke off and, tight-lipped, stared ahead. That was how she sat for the drive back to the Belmar exit, unmoving, damn near unblinking. When he turned onto the highway that eventually became Ocean Street, she broke her silence. "It's wrong."

He didn't look at her or encourage her to go on, but she did anyway.

"Accepting 'perks' from business owners, intimidating people, using your job to avoid the consequences of your actions—it's all wrong. Whether it's a fifty-cent cup of coffee or a two-hundred-dollar ticket, it's an abuse of your position."

"Two-hundred-dollar ticket, my ass. He

probably would've taken me to jail for reckless driving," Mitch muttered. Again not the response she wanted to hear.

"Police officers should be held to a higher standard than everyone else. They're supposed to uphold the law—every law. Not bend it and twist it to their own advantage. But Taylor, Billy Starrett and all those cops this morning think they're above the law, and you're just like them."

The insult rankled, but Mitch ignored it. "You're being ridiculous." He refused to feel guilty about the troopers letting him slide on speeding infractions. There were so many more important things going on that driving a few miles over the limit didn't begin to compare.

She opened her mouth, about to really unload on him, he suspected, then clamped it shut again. She was grinding her teeth so hard by the time he turned into the Sand Dollar that she'd probably worn down her molars.

He parked in front of his apartment, grabbed the cobbler from the back and put up the Mustang's top. "You'll have to excuse me if I don't see you to your door. I can stand only so much hypocritical bull at once."

After letting himself into his apartment, he closed and locked the door, put the cobbler in the refrigerator, then returned to the living room to draw the drapes. She was still standing next to the Mustang, looking innocent and troubled. If there was one thing Jennifer Burton wasn't, it was innocent.

And if there was one thing she definitely was, it was trouble. With a capital T.

Chapter 4

Later that night, Jessica lay in her bed, only a dim light burning on the night table. She vented to Jen, but her sister was noticeably lacking in sympathy.

"Why did you go to dinner with him anyway?"

"Because they're keeping an eye on me. If I hadn't gone with him, he would have followed me. It just seemed silly." It was a weak excuse, and Jessica hurried on before Jen could point that out. "Besides, I never would have had the best barbecue ever if not for him."

"Oh, you went to Studdard's."

"No. Down Home Q. It's owned by a guy

Mitch and Taylor played football with in high school—Willis Pickering."

"I've never heard Taylor mention him or the restaurant. Where is it?"

Jessica didn't know the street names but was able to give a general location.

"Well, that explains it," Jen said. "It's in the wrong part of town for Police Chief Taylor Burton."

"So he's a racist, too?"

"Racist, sexist, elitist. Have you noticed there are no black, female or Latino police officers in Belmar?"

So far, Jessica had really noticed only three officers: Taylor himself, the kid cop and Mitch. Handsome, sexy, sometimes intriguing, sometimes damn near charming, why-shouldn't-I-get-away-with-breaking-the-law-I'm-a-cop Mitch. Squeezing her eyes shut, she shifted the cell phone to her other ear. "How the hell did you fall for this guy, Jen? Why did it take you so long to see him for what he really is?"

There was silence for a moment, an odd emptiness actually devoid of sound, then Jen sighed. "He was so very good at pretending and I was so very much in love and so very much in denial. I didn't want to believe…I just kept insisting…and then it was too late." Emotion rushed into her voice, giving it strength. "Don't make the same mistake I did, Jess. Don't let Mitch Lassiter convince you that he's a better person than he really is. He's one of Taylor's men. Period."

Jessica scoffed, though not very convincingly. "Trust me, the only thing less likely than me falling for Mitch is me falling for Taylor." Or Billy Starrett. Or the kid cop.

Hmm. Mitch was definitely the best of the bunch.

"You would have seen through Taylor from the start," Jen said softly, wistfully. "You've always been a better judge of people than me. I just wanted…"

To fall in love. Get married. Have a houseful of babies. Live happily ever after. It was all Jen had ever wanted, just as all Jessica had wanted was everything else. A career, travel, excitement, opportunity. She'd thought falling in love and marriage might happen at some distant point in the future, when or if living for months at a time in Hong Kong, Beijing or Tokyo ever lost its appeal.

"He probably would have fooled me, too," Jessica said. Granted, the mere sight of him that morning had made her skin crawl, but it hadn't been like meeting a stranger. She'd had the benefit of Jen's hard-earned knowledge.

"Probably not, but thanks for saying so." Jen's voice sounded better, less heartbroken. "If they're watching you, how are you going to get into Taylor's house to search?"

"Don't worry about that. I have a plan."

"You always do. That's why you're the big sister. I'll check in with you later, Jess. Take care."

Jessica flipped the phone shut, then curled up on her side. Jen was too trusting by far. The only plan Jessica had was to *get* a plan, and it wasn't as if she could run out and buy one. But she would come up with something. Jen was counting on her, and while Jessica felt as if she'd let her down before, she swore it wouldn't happen again.

Missing her sister fiercely, she dozed off and on, her sleep disturbed by fitful dreams of events long past—the first time she'd faced down the neighborhood bully on Jen's behalf. The friendships she'd rejected because they hadn't been extended to Jen, as well. The countless times she'd helped her twin out by posing as her for dates she didn't want to go on, tests she hadn't studied for, even a job interview she'd dreaded.

She awoke feeling cranky and poorly rested though, according to the alarm clock, she'd slept nearly twelve hours. Hip aching, she reached under the covers and found the cell phone, slipped from her grasp at some time during the night. She moved it to the night table, then stared at the ceiling.

All their lives she'd protected her sister, and yet she'd been the one to bring danger into Jen's life. That damn cruise…she'd thought she was doing Jen a favor. A free weeklong Caribbean cruise—who wouldn't have been happy for an opportunity like that? But if not for the cruise, Jen never would have met Taylor. Never would have married him. Never would have gotten her heart broken. Never would have—

The jangle of the phone startled her. There was no caller ID to check and no answering machine to pick up. After the fourth ring, Jessica vowed to take care of both that day, then picked up the receiver. "Hello."

"Jennifer, it's Starla Starrett." The woman's voice was Southern and a tad shrill. Jessica wouldn't have liked her based on nothing more than that, though thanks to Jen, she knew so much more. "Do you remember me? My husband works with Taylor?"

"Of course I remember you. My car was washed off the road and I almost drowned, but I don't have amnesia." After a pause, she deliberately added, "At least not about anything besides that night."

Starla's laugh sounded phony. She *was* phony, Jen said, from her peroxided hair to her fake boobs, all the way down to her liposuctioned thighs and the fake diamond on her toe ring. "Well, that's a relief. I was so glad when Billy told me you were back. We were all so worried about you."

Liar.

"Anyway, I was calling to see if we could meet for lunch. Maybe at the Beach Club."

Lunch with plastic Starla. Oh, goody. Wouldn't that fit perfectly into what already promised to be a less than pleasant day—and she wasn't even out of bed yet. But who knew? Maybe she would learn something, like whose idea this invitation was, because no doubt it was just another way for Taylor to keep tabs on her.

"Sure, I'd like that. What time?"

"Would an hour give you enough time?"

Jessica's eyes crossed as she stuck out her tongue at the phone. She could throw on a T-shirt and jeans and run her fingers through her hair, brush her teeth and add a touch of lipstick and be out the door in under five minutes. It wouldn't bother her in the least. "I think I can manage that," she said drily.

"Great! I'll see you there."

After hanging up, Jessica actually did more

than she'd considered—a shower, full makeup, jewelry, perfume—and left the apartment. She'd found a dress in the closet that wasn't too drab—cinnamon in color, sleeveless, fitted in the bodice and flaring to end midcalf. It wasn't her style, but at least there wasn't a ruffle in sight.

She walked out of the apartment, and the kid cop, standing in the shade and talking to a young woman in shorts and swimsuit bra, jumped to attention. A creepy feeling crawled down her spine at the way he looked at her, like a predator eyeing its prey. She resisted the urge to dart back inside, out of his line of sight, and went to the car instead.

The Beach Club was located, appropriately, on the beach at the end of Ocean Street. The building was designed to resemble a tropical house—large, airy, with more windows than exterior walls. Paddle fans supplemented the gulf breeze on the wide verandas, and giant umbrellas shaded tables in the courtyard. It was one of *the* places to dine in Belmar, so Jen and Taylor had been regulars. At high noon on a Thursday—

on any day, she'd bet—it was crowded, both with visitors to the beach and locals.

Wondering how difficult it would be to pick Starla out of the bunch, Jessica climbed the broad steps to the front veranda and was halfway to the door when a shrill call came from the corner. "Jennifer!"

Oh, yeah, that must be Starla. No one's hair came in that collection of shades naturally, just as very few women as petite as she had a chest like that naturally. Her clothes were expensive, her makeup overdone, her jewelry big enough and abundant enough to verge into tackiness and she smelled like a million bucks—or at least a hundred and fifty bucks an ounce—when she enveloped Jessica in a hug.

"It's so good to see you! Why, we were just all out of our minds when you turned up missing after the storm. Taylor was sick with worry over what had happened to you. You have to sit down and tell me all about your adventures."

Sneaking into her husband's house, rifling through his belongings, taking something important, running for her life, getting hit a few times and held underwater before washing away with the rushing current… *Adventures* was one way to describe it.

Nightmare was another.

There were four chairs at Starla's table. She'd chosen the one that faced the entrance—the better to see and be seen. Jessica sat opposite her, with her back to the other customers. The better to not face their curious gazes. Behind Starla, the beach stretched out, smooth and sandy, as far as the eye could see. Waves rolled in off the gulf, fairly tame compared to what Jessica was used to but big enough to satisfy the swimmers and kids on boogie boards.

It was a lovely scene. Take away the restaurant, the parking lot filled with cars, the businessmen, the "women who lunch" and the tourists, and she would be content. Move the whole thing eighteen hundred miles west to California, and she'd be happy.

Get rid of the kid cop, too, she added when a low whistle in the parking lot drew her gaze that way.

He was flirting with two girls coming in from the beach. Neither appeared a day over fifteen, and both met his attention with looks of revulsion.

"That Jimmy Ray," Starla said with a laugh. "He thinks he's God's gift to the women of Mississippi. Someday he probably will be, but he's still got a few years of growing to do."

Jessica looked at Jimmy Ray again, then at Starla to see if she was joking. She wasn't. Even if he grew from then until the end of eternity, his ick factor would still be off the scale. No woman was going to appreciate him, except maybe the teenage version of Starla.

"Well. So." Starla smiled brightly. "Where've you been? What've you been doing?"

"Recuperating." Which might be too big a word for Starla. "I hit my head when the car washed off the road." *Lie.* "I almost drowned. I had to recover."

"Where? And why didn't you call Taylor?"

"My sister came from Hong Kong to be with me. I, uh, needed her more than I did Taylor. You know—family, a woman, all that."

"Oh, yeah, when I'm sick, I'd much rather

have my mama than Billy taking care of me."
Starla's blue eyes, as fake as everything else,
sharpened as she leaned forward. The action
pushed her breasts together and up so far that
they surely must have interfered with her breathing. "But why didn't you let Taylor know you
were all right, hon? He was really beside
himself, thinking you were dead and all. It just
about broke my heart to watch him."

Jessica's smile was thin. When Jen had told
Taylor she was leaving him—after she'd rented
the apartment, after she'd moved most of her
stuff out—his response had been simple. Not
How can we fix this? Not *I love you, please don't
go.* Just *What will people think?*

"Taylor and I are separated, Starla. We're
probably not ever getting back together."

"Oh, I don't know," Starla said with a coy
smile. "When he wants something, he doesn't
give up until he's got it."

Her words were probably meant as encouragement, but they struck Jessica as ominous. Taylor
wanted something, all right—the evidence that

Jen had taken. How far was he willing to go to get it? Intimidation was a given. Threats, sure. Misuse of authority. Blackmail. Coercion.

Probably murder.

Jessica's stomach flip-flopped at the thought.

The entire meal continued in that fashion—questions about the night of the storm, positive comments about Taylor, then a brief spate about fashion, movies or shopping. Jessica had no doubt that Starla had been coached on what questions to ask; the only thoughts that made it out of the empty space of her brain on their own were utterly innocuous. If she weren't pretty—enhanced or not—there wasn't a soul alive who'd have a use for her.

There were only two good things about the meal, Jessica decided when it was over: the food was decent for a trendy beach place, and soon after they'd ordered, Jimmy Ray had climbed into his car and driven away. He was probably off to have lunch at a strip club, if there was one nearby, ogling the women while drooling onto his food.

"Well, hon, this has been fun and all, but I'm gonna have to get moving. I have an appointment. Got to get my nails touched up." Starla waggled ten fake nails done in hot-pink in the air. "We'll have to get together again, maybe do a couples thing at the country club or something. I'll give you a call."

"Sure. Just give me time to find a date."

Starla blinked, her expression slack, then laughed. "You're so funny, Jennifer. I never noticed that before. See you."

Jessica tilted her head back and closed her eyes, letting the breeze from the fan blow the tension from her face. She routinely facilitated complex contracts between people from very different cultures without getting the slightest bit stressed, but ninety minutes with Starla had left her feeling whipped. She needed a couple of stiff drinks from the bar to recoup—better yet, one of the decadent chocolate desserts the next table had ordered—but she didn't have time. With Jimmy Ray off wherever, this was her best chance to head to Taylor's.

The waitress hadn't brought a check and was nowhere to be seen. Jessica tucked a twenty under her glass, stood up...and locked gazes with Mitch. Damn it, how had he gotten so close without her noticing? He sat only five tables away, a glass of iced tea in front of him, his long legs stretched out so his boots rested against the railing. He looked better in the drab uniform than any man had a right to—and he didn't look happy to see her.

The feeling was mutual. That little quiver chasing down her spine was just annoyance, nothing more.

Leaving meant walking directly past him, something she'd rather not do at the moment, but sitting down again somehow felt like giving in. She was ready to go, so by God, she was going. If he wanted to follow, he could.

Shoulders rigid, she walked the length of the veranda, her gaze never breaking with his until she passed him. Resting her hand on the hot wood of the railing, she went down one step, then impulsively turned around and returned to his table. He was watching the waves and sipping tea through a straw—and continued to do so as she stood there, patiently waiting for his attention. She would have bet he could outwait her, but after a moment or two, his features taut with irritation, he glanced her way—not at her face but somewhere around her middle.

"How much of the taxpayers' money is Taylor paying you to follow me?"

Slowly his gaze moved upward, his eyes even darker than she remembered. "Why? You going to offer me more?"

"Maybe." That was exactly what she'd had in mind. If Taylor could buy him, then maybe she could, too. At least for a few hours.

A slow grin curved his mouth, but there was nothing amused about it. "You don't have enough money."

"People like you always have their price."

"People like me?"

"The ethically and morally challenged. Those who consider themselves above the law."

His gaze hardened. "Oh, yeah. The ones who bend it and twist it to their advantage."

She refused to let even an ounce of guilt over last night's conversation creep in. "How much?"

"Like I said, you can't afford me."

"You have no idea what I can afford." She made very good money and very smart invest-ments, and together she and Jen had been the sole heirs to their parents' estates. It would take a few days, but she could probably put together enough cash to satisfy even Taylor's greed.

She slipped into one of the empty chairs. "You're... what? Thirty-three? Thirty-four? With a nothing little job in a nothing little town, and you wouldn't even have that if not for your old buddy Taylor."

"You gonna take me away from all this?" He gestured with his glass.

"No. But I can make it easier for you to afford a little of it for yourself. And you don't even have to do anything. You take Taylor's money, you give him bogus reports and you stay hell and gone away from me."

There was another of those nasty little grins. "And here I've been enjoying your company so much."

Then, abruptly, he leaned toward her. She automatically scooted back before she could stop herself. "Tell me something, Mrs. Burton. What is it you're wanting to do that you don't want your husband to know about?"

Uh-oh. Warmth flooded her face. She'd made a mistake. She should have just walked past and let him follow her home. Instead she'd roused his suspicions. He would probably make sure she never escaped surveillance... unless he was as corrupt as Taylor, in which case he would probably ask for some ungodly sum for his help.

Some foolish part of her really didn't want him to be as corrupt as Taylor.

"I just want to be left alone." It wasn't a great answer but the best she could come up with. "I don't like being followed everywhere. I can't even open my curtains at home because that little creep is out there. Call me strange, but being stalked just doesn't turn me on."

Bad choice of words, she realized the instant they were out. The muscles in Mitch's jaw clenched as his gaze dropped lower, to her mouth.

His eyes turned hard in a different way, and smoky, and her chest tightened so completely that she couldn't draw a breath to save her life.

His movements slow and deliberate, he set his glass down, pushed his chair back and stood up. For a moment he just looked at her, then he slid his sunglasses on. They didn't lessen the intensity of his stare one bit. As he turned away, he gritted out something, then walked to the stairs, where he waited for her to follow.

She got slowly to her feet. His words had been beneath his breath, harshly formed and not intended for her ears, but she'd understood them anyway. At least she thought she had.

I could turn you on, and it wouldn't cost a damn thing.

Dear God, why wasn't she running in the opposite direction?

What was she up to?

The thought kept running through Mitch's mind as he followed Jennifer on a circuitous route back to the apartment. She made brief stops on the way—the bookstore, the movie rental store, the post office—each time pretending she didn't see him right there waiting. Now she was in the liquor store. He watched through the large plate-glass windows as she moved slowly along the wine aisles, occasionally picking up a bottle, studying the label and smiling before returning it to the rack.

He'd been in town five weeks before the hurricane and had met her his second day back at a welcome party Taylor had thrown at the country club. He'd thought she was pretty, too quiet for his tastes and for Taylor's, too. Soon after, she had moved in next door, and running into her coming or going had become a pretty regular occurrence. But not once had he ever watched her the way he did now. Not once had he even noticed her as a woman, much less a desirable woman. What had happened between the night of the hurricane and the night she'd returned?

And why had she returned? What was she up to?

No doubt she'd told the truth. *I don't like being followed everywhere.* Who wanted their every movement scrutinized, regardless of whether they had something to hide?

But there was something more to her desire for privacy, something having to do with her return to Belmar. Maybe she had a boyfriend there, someone she'd hooked up with before the hurricane, someone unwilling to leave town. The idea was distasteful. Much about Mitch's life was distasteful lately, but he forced himself to consider it. Who in town was foolish enough to risk an affaire with the police chief's wife? Who was foolish enough to choose Belmar over a woman like Jennifer?

No one came to mind, though Mitch couldn't be sure if he was eliminating prospects because they weren't really prospects or because he didn't want to think of Jennifer being that involved with another man.

She had unfinished business, she'd said, and his immediate thought had been Taylor and divorce. But Taylor wasn't worried about a divorce…and yet he wanted to know every move she made. So what *was* he worried about? Did she have something on him? Did he consider her a threat in some way?

Mitch wished *he* had more on Taylor than he currently did.

She came out of the liquor store, a tall brown bag cradled in one arm, and walked to her car with an easy, graceful stride. He would bet she'd studied dance or gymnastics as a kid. Her movements were fluid, the gentle sway of her hips womanly and enticing.

Gritting his teeth, he followed her car out of the parking lot and onto Ocean, where Jimmy Ray pulled alongside and gave him a big ole grin and a wave before cutting between their cars. A little creep, she'd called him, and it was a pretty accurate assessment.

Mitch drove to a pay phone, this one in the poorer section of town outside a run-down grocery store. Though the customers passing by viewed his patrol unit with suspicion, most of them relaxed when they recognized him. Given a choice, Taylor would bulldoze this part of town and relocate its citizens elsewhere, and most of the department felt the same way. Mitch was the exception.

Apparently midweek afternoons were quiet in the strip bar. For all the background noise, Rick might have been alone. He sounded bored and sleepy—he got that way with nothing to do. "What's up?"

"The price of gas. The price of a good time. The price of a conscience."

"Sounds like you're not having fun down there in the land of official corruption."

"I've had better times. Can you do me a favor?"

"As long as it doesn't involve leaving town in the next couple days."

"Nah, just a phone call or two." Rick had more contacts in more places than anyone else Mitch knew. "I want to know how Jennifer Burton's financials look."

It was easy to imagine Rick scrawling the name on a napkin as he spelled it aloud. "J-e-n-i-f-f-e-r?" He wasn't the best speller, but he paid great attention to other details. It made him good at everything he did.

"Two n's, one f. She banks at First Union here in Belmar, but I bet she's still got accounts in California, too."

"Why do you care?"

"Because she offered me a deal—Taylor pays me to watch her, she'll pay me to leave her alone and lie to him. This was right after she called me ethically and morally challenged." It still stung, more than he wanted to acknowledge even to Rick.

His brother was about as sympathetic as he ever got. "Job's turning out tougher than you expected, isn't it? That's what you get for having expectations. You want to see if she can really afford to pay you off?"

"I'm curious."

"What's she trying to hide from her old man?"

"I'm curious about that, too."

"I'll see what I can find out. Give me a call in a day or two."

"I will." He was about to say goodbye when Rick spoke again.

"Hey, Mitch? Be careful."

Funny. A week ago that admonishment would

have immediately brought to mind Taylor, jovial and friendly when things were going his way and dangerous when they weren't. This afternoon the image that appeared was Jennifer's.

"I will," he replied.

As much as he was able.

The rest of the afternoon passed more slowly than usual. He wrote a dozen tickets, broke up a bar fight between two drunken tourists who'd taken a liking to the same waitress and worked two minor accidents. It was past his usual quitting time when he returned to the station, parking in the lot out back and entering through the rear door. The first thing he heard as he approached the squad room was Starla Starrett's voice.

Billy Starrett thought any man who didn't openly envy him his wife was just hiding behind his jealousy. Mitch figured a smart man was more likely to pity him than envy him. Starla was pretty enough in an artificial sort of way, but she was about as shallow as a raindrop. Her idea of current affairs was who the current crop of celebrities was dating, and she'd never strung together an intelligent thought in the twenty-some years he'd known her.

And since her last implants, if she ever fell facedown, she would never get up without help.

She was tempting fate by leaning over a desk shared by several younger officers, either not noticing or not caring that their gazes never veered higher than her chest. Her smile widened when she saw him. "Mitch Lassiter. No bigger than Belmar is, how is it I never see you out and about?"

Because I see you first. He didn't say it, of course, because his grandmother had taught him better. Besides, Starla might be dumber than dirt, but she wasn't a bad person. She flirted with every male on the radar, but it never went beyond that. She was coy and cloying and had never aspired to any goal besides being pretty and sexy, but it worked for her. The girl who'd grown up dirt-poor now lived in the most expensive neighborhood in town and drove a cherry-red Z3. Why change her methods now?

"You come to meet Billy?"

She waved crimson-tipped fingers toward

Taylor's closed door and answered with an air of importance. "Actually, I had a nice little talk with the chief."

"Reporting on your lunch date?"

She smiled prettily but didn't answer.

Had Jennifer known every word she'd said would be repeated to Taylor? Probably. She was neither shallow nor dumb. She didn't dress like an expensive hooker, didn't flirt as naturally as breathing—hell, didn't flirt at all, as far as he could tell—and her voice didn't grate like fingernails on a chalkboard. She had the kind of voice that could fuel a man's fantasies...or jab a hole in his pride. *Ethically and morally challenged, my ass.*

Starla laid her hand on his arm to get his attention. "My cousin, Sue Ann, is coming for a visit next week. You remember her from school? 'Cause she sure remembers you. How about I set you two up for dinner one night? She'll make it worth your time."

He remembered Sue Ann. Runaround Sue, the boys had called her, after some old song. She hadn't been his type back then, and he couldn't imagine that she'd changed enough that she was now. "I don't think so, Starla. I'm kind of busy with other things."

"Oh." She glanced at the young cops, still staring at her, then gave him a wink. "I understand."

He didn't, until she went on.

"Taylor's got you pulling extra duty with you-know-who, doesn't he? But I bet Jimmy Ray or one of these boys would be happy to fill in for a night, wouldn't you, boys?"

"You bet," one of them answered without even knowing what he was agreeing to. She could have asked him to jump off the roof and he would have said yes just as quickly.

Mitch shook his head. It was bad enough that Jimmy Ray was hanging around during the day. He damn well didn't want him or anyone else stalking Jennifer at night. That was *his* job. "Sorry. Maybe next time."

Hoping he could get out without running into Taylor, Mitch headed for the locker room. His hand was on the doorknob when his luck ran out.

"Hey, Bubba, come on in."

After taking a moment to clear the exasperation from his face, Mitch turned to face Taylor, standing in his office doorway. Though the previous chiefs had never worn uniforms, Taylor did, probably because he liked the four shiny gold stars on each collar point and the way the leather of his gun belt creaked when he moved. Or because it amused him to wear the uniform of the law while breaking the law.

Mitch went into the office and closed the door but didn't sit down. Taylor did.

"So? What's the report from last night?"

Resentment churned inside him. He didn't like this job or being used to spy on anyone. He didn't like Taylor's smugness and he especially didn't like reporting to him on Jennifer's activities. But he kept that inside and shrugged. "About six-fifteen, she went to dinner at Down Home Q. She got home a couple hours later and didn't go out again."

Taylor sneered. "Down Home Q? How the hell does she even know that place exists? I damn sure never took her there."

Mitch shrugged. He wasn't about to admit that it was his idea or that they'd gone together. If Taylor found out, then he'd come up with a plausible explanation. But what were the odds of that? Jennifer had guessed right that Willis didn't like Taylor. He would never volunteer anything to the police, and neither would his usual customers.

"Jeez, I can't believe she'd pass up Studdard's for a dive like that. She probably did it just to annoy me. Did she talk to anyone?"

"Just the waitress."

"Who are the waitresses out there?"

"Mostly Willis's daughters and nieces."

"So he's still around. Huh."

Mitch's head was hurting, and thanks to the bar fight, he smelled like a dirty ashtray. All he wanted was to go home, take a shower and forget about the job and Taylor and everything else for a while. He could manage going home and the shower, but even though he would be off the clock in another couple minutes, he wasn't going to be off the job.

He scowled. "Can I go now?"

Taylor, gazing off into the distance, drew his attention back to him. "Yeah. If anything of interest happens tonight, you can reach me on my cell. Otherwise, stop by in the morning."

As Mitch left the office for the locker room, he wryly noted that his definition regarding Jennifer and *interesting* varied widely from Taylor's. He found watching her walk of interest. Watching her smile. Listening to her talk. And Taylor wanted to know if she...what? Met with another man? Tried to sell off, damage or destroy his property behind his back? Had a sit-down with any federal agents with an interest in police corruption? Better yet, with a hit man willing to help her avoid the nastiness of a divorce?

He stamped his time card at the clock mounted next to the locker room door, then made a beeline for the rear door. This time he made it out without anyone speaking to him. Five minutes later, he was home, stripping off his uniform. The belt, gun belt, badge and nameplate went on the dresser, the bulletproof vest and boots into the closet and everything else into the hamper.

He was one of the few Belmar officers who wore a vest—Jimmy Ray was another—but then, he knew things the others didn't.

He'd showered and dressed in cotton shorts and a T-shirt when a knock sounded at the door. Combing his damp hair back, he opened it without checking the peephole and found himself face-to-face with Jennifer.

She didn't smile in greeting. "Now that Taylor's baby-faced minion is gone, I'm going to the beach for a picnic and a swim."

She was dressed more elegantly for the beach than anyone he'd seen. She wore khaki shorts, knee-length, pressed and creased, and a white sleeveless shirt, also pressed. Her sandals were linen and jute, beaded, and better suited for dining or shopping than tramping through the sand.

He didn't have a choice but to tag along. Even if he did, there was no question that he would go. The dark shadow of a swimsuit showing underneath the white blouse made sure of that.

Still, he made an effort to sound grudging. "Let me get—"

"I've got everything."

"Beer?"

"Better—wine. And food and sunscreen and towels and a blanket. I'll even let you drive."

"Let me get my gun—or do you have one of those, too?"

She said nothing, but her mouth flattened.

He retrieved his .45, clipping the holster onto his waistband and pulling his shirt down to cover it, then shoved his feet into his most broken-down running shoes. When he joined her on the sidewalk, she was waiting impatiently with a huge canvas bag slung over one shoulder and a small ice chest next to her.

He waited until they were on their way to ask, "If Jimmy Ray is Taylor's baby-faced minion, what does that make me?"

She slid on a pair of dark glasses before shooting him a sidelong look. "I don't think you want to know."

No. He didn't.

"Which beach?" he asked instead.

The question stumped her. "I don't know.

Taylor prefers to do his swimming at the country club pool. You pick."

"I can count the number of times I've been to the country club on one hand. The prom my junior and senior years and the welcome-back party Taylor—you and Taylor," some little devil made him say, "gave. The night we met. And here we are, headed off to the beach together."

She didn't respond. That was all right. He hadn't expected her to. Rick was right—not having expectations was easier.

It was simple enough to pick his favorite stretch of beach. It was in the county, about six miles from town, and its parking lot consisted of a cleared area with weeds growing through the crushed shell. There was no trail leading to the sand, just a rugged hike across thirty feet, but it was quiet and private.

This evening was no exception. When they crested the small rise that separated lot from sand, there wasn't another person in sight. It was just the two of them, the seagulls and the water.

And that was one hell of a dangerous combination.

Chapter 5

"I wouldn't have figured you for the beach type."

Jessica glanced at Mitch as she shook out the pricey coverlet she'd taken from Jen's bed. Her thorough search of the apartment the day before should have turned up a battered old quilt for picnicking; their mother had had one and had made one for each of them. Jessica's was pieced from squares of worn denim from her old jeans, and Jen's from old dresses, all flowers and pastels. Even as kids, she'd favored more feminine clothes than Jessica.

But there'd been no sign of the quilt. Was it

at Taylor's house? Or had he "persuaded" Jen to get rid of it?

"I'm from California," she said with a shrug. Kicking off her shoes, she sat down on the cover and began unpacking the tote.

"Yeah, but there's California beach types, and then there's California…"

He broke off to search for the word and she waited. Obviously he was implying that she was the other type. What would that be? City? Snobby? Snooty?

He didn't finish, though, but settled for a shrug instead. That was all right. She didn't think a lot of him, either. Though she spent a lot of time thinking of him.

"For the record," she said as she squirted sunscreen onto her palm, then began rubbing it over her arm, "I am definitely a beach type. My sister and I grew up less than two miles from the ocean. In the summer we were there at least four or five times a week. We learned to swim and to surf—" Abruptly she remembered that Jen had never mastered surfing. After a few lessons, she'd sworn there were better ways to die than drowning and she had never gone near a board again.

The memory made Jessica immeasurably sad.

"You learned to swim and surf," Mitch prodded.

She blinked, wondering how long she'd zoned out, then forced herself to concentrate. "Actually, Jessica learned. I tried but decided working on my tan was a better use of my time and natural abilities."

Wrong words to say when she was unbuttoning her shirt. All he did was lower his gaze to her hands, and discomfort swept through her. It was silly. There was nothing the least bit immodest about Jen's one-piece swimsuit. The biggest prude in the world wouldn't be embarrassed by the retro-look, shirred-front, built-in bra and boy-cut legs. Jessica had worn far less in front of total strangers on beaches around the world without a second thought.

But Mitch wasn't a stranger. He was someone she couldn't afford to get involved with. Someone she couldn't stop wanting to get involved with.

Though her hands were unsteady, she forced the last button open, then shrugged out of the blouse, laying it aside. Rising to her feet, she unzipped the shorts, stepped out of them and set them to the side, as well. Goose bumps immediately appeared on her arms and legs, despite the temperature that was well into the eighties.

"Looks like you gave up the tanning." His voice was deeper than usual, hoarser.

Hers was unsteady, breathy. "Yeah, well, teenage girls eventually get smart." The only color she had now was the pale gold that came naturally and the pink warming her cheeks.

She left her sunglasses on the blanket, then walked to the water's edge, all too aware of his gaze on her. The waves were gentle, the water tepid as it washed over her feet, drizzling tiny streams of sand between her toes.

She turned to the east, strolling in ankle-deep water, watching the seagulls swoop and dive, letting the familiar scents and sounds seep through her. She was feeling pretty relaxed when Mitch fell into step beside her, enough that the only tension he roused was the unwise but still pleasant sexual-awareness sort.

"This is called Posey's Park," he commented, gesturing around them. "Not much of a park, but the Posey family didn't require much to be happy. For years they owned a long stretch here. In the fifties and sixties, developers kept trying to buy it, but the old man turned them down. His children thought that when he died, they'd sell it and make a few million, but he left it to the county instead, and they've never bothered to do anything with it."

"Which suits you just fine."

He shrugged.

"Are there any Poseys still around?"

"Most of them moved away after the old man destroyed their dreams of riches. The last one in the area died while I was in college."

She glanced sideways at him. "Your grand-mother?"

He nodded. "She was a Posey by marriage. Her name was Lou—short for something, she'd say, but she never told anyone what. I found out when she died it was Louella."

She bent to pick up a shell, then brushed sand from it as they walked. "My mother's name was Ella. Everyone called her Ellie." She'd been smart and fun and funny, the best mom in the neighborhood. She had encouraged Jessica to have her career and Jen to have her family and had been role model to them both.

"What are you doing here?"

The abrupt change in topic unsettled her, but she tried not to show it. She wiped the last grain of sand from the shell, studied it a moment, then drew back her arm and lobbed it into the water. "I like the beach," she replied evenly. "I like picnics at the beach. They bring back better times."

It wasn't the answer he wanted, and it showed in the tightening of his jaw. "In Belmar. Why did you come back? What unfinished business do you have here? What are you up to?"

Of all his questions, the last was the most worrisome. The others could be spurred by mere curiosity, but the last was brought about by suspicion. He knew she had something to hide, knew it involved Taylor, knew it couldn't be good for Taylor. What would he do if she told him the truth? Turn her over to his boss? Help her? Dismiss her?

She didn't know, and in this case, not knowing could be fatal. *Don't trust anyone,* Jen had warned and she'd named Mitch in particular.

"I'm not up to anything," she said, aiming for a breezy tone. "Belmar has been my home for three years. I'm comfortable here—at least, I would be if people weren't scrutinizing my every move. I have some big decisions to make and I might as well be someplace familiar while I make them."

"Los Angeles was your home for twenty-five years. It must be a hell of a lot more familiar."

"It's also got a lot of sad memories now that my parents are gone." They'd been such a big part of her and Jen's lives. Even as adults, she and Jen had lived within a few miles of home and they'd seen their parents at least two or three times a week. They had vacationed together, celebrated together. After they'd died—their mother first, their father eight months later—life had seemed out of balance. She had begun making longer and longer trips to Asia, and Jen had gone off and married Taylor.

"What decisions?"

She stopped walking and looked over her shoulder. They'd gone so far that the blanket and ice chest were barely distinguishable in the distance. If someone happened to come along, he could help himself to a good dinner and a very nice bottle of wine. Then she would have an excuse for canceling the picnic and returning home to hide in Jen's little apartment.

"Who's asking?" she asked. "You or Taylor? Are you just keeping track of my movements or are you also repeating everything I say to him, like Starla?"

"You figured that out."

"A brain-dead person would have figured that out."

The breeze rustled his hair, blowing a strand over his forehead that he impatiently pushed back. "As far as Taylor knows, we haven't spoken."

That left her almost as surprised as skeptical.

"He thinks we went to dinner last night and didn't speak for nearly two hours?"

Mitch's scowl narrowed his gaze and etched lines across his face. "He thinks you went to dinner alone and that I watched you from a distance. He doesn't know we talked then or at the Beach Club or the apartment or the grocery store parking lot. He damn sure doesn't know we're talking now."

She had no doubt that Mitch could lie with the best of them, but something about his manner made her believe him this time. That was why he'd chosen Down Home Q instead of Taylor's favorite, Studdard's, and why he'd brought her all the way out here instead of heading for the beach in town. No one was likely to see them together or, in the case of the Pickerings, admit it if they did.

She started back in the direction they'd come, and he matched her stride for stride. "You and Taylor are friends," she said, not intending the words to sound like an accusation but saying them that way anyway.

"We have been."

Interesting phrasing. Was he implying that they no longer were? Or merely lying, hoping she would think that?

"Taylor and I are adversaries, which makes you and me adversaries, which means I couldn't trust you if I wanted to. And I don't." Those last three words, said with extra emphasis, were more for herself than him, she feared.

"Let me ask a different question. What does Taylor think you're up to that requires twenty-four-hour-a-day surveillance?"

"Twenty-four hours? Is there someone sitting out there in the dark all night—" what a creepy thought "—or do you stay awake until Jimmy Ray takes over after breakfast?"

"There's no one out there," he said drily, "and I do sleep from time to time."

In the room right next to hers, with only a thin wall separating them. If he had a girlfriend over, she would probably know. If she had a man over…of course he would know, because he was the only man who'd tempted her in way too long.

To avoid where that line of thought would end—bed, his or hers, both of them naked—she cleared the huskiness from her throat and returned to the original subject. "I don't have a clue why Taylor thinks I require surveillance. Maybe he's hoping to catch me with some guy so he can use it in a divorce. As if he hasn't been with plenty of other women."

It had broken Jen's heart to discover that he'd been unfaithful to her. If it had just been toward the end, when the marriage was falling apart, she could have dealt with that. But, no, he'd been sleeping with other women long before that. Whatever Taylor wanted, Taylor got, and to hell with whoever might get hurt in the process.

A strangled sound came from Mitch at her last words, and she glanced his way to see that he was blushing. It should have looked ridiculous on a man like him, but instead there was something boyish and charming about it.

"What?" she asked, annoyed with herself for being charmed. "You thought I was too naive or stupid to know about his other women?"

"Not at all. I just figured…hell, I didn't know for sure about them until after you disappeared."

Billy Starrett had known. So had Starla and most of Taylor's friends. *We have been friends.* Past tense. Weren't anymore, perhaps, or he would have been more in the loop.

Then something else struck her: he was embarrassed to find out that she knew about Taylor's infidelity. It was an uncomfortable subject for him. Could he actually have one intact moral inside him? And if there was one, could there be others?

She didn't want to consider it, be tempted by it. As they drew even with the blanket, she veered to her left. "I'm going for a swim."

He didn't follow her in but returned to the blanket. She waded into the water, slipping under when it became deep enough, coming up and heading due south with strong, steady strokes. As long as there weren't sharks in the water, she could paddle around offshore forever before getting tired.

Then she glanced back to the beach, where Mitch was lying on the blanket, leaning on one elbow. Who cared about sharks in the water when the baddest of them all was waiting for her on the sand?

"We should be going."

The sun was setting, lost in a haze of clouds, the air a few degrees cooler and Mitch's stomach was full. He would have been satisfied to stay where he was, enjoying the quiet broken only by the sounds of the gulf, but instead he sat up, worked the cork back into the wine bottle, then handed it, neck first, to Jennifer. "Yeah. We should."

Dinner had been good—Caesar salad and chicken salad on croissants, followed by chocolate cake covered with a sticky whiskey sauce, served on real plates with silverware, crystal and linen napkins. A far cry from the picnics he and Lou had shared on this same beach. They'd usually brought bologna sandwiches wrapped in paper towels that doubled as napkins, a bag of potato chips and ice-cold cans of Coke—easy to fix and leaving little trash to pack out, she'd always declared.

Taylor had said Jennifer couldn't cook, but she'd claimed the Caesar dressing as her own recipe, and the chicken salad had been cool, creamy and crunchy. And the cake...he'd probably eaten enough of that to get a buzz from the whiskey. Were Taylor's standards impossibly high, did he find some prestige in eating every meal out at no cost to himself or was he just a hypercritical lying bastard?

She packed the dishes, then rose gracefully to her feet, unknotting the towel that had dried around her. Mitch stood up, too, moving the tote and ice chest from the quilt, then walking away a few yards to shake out the sand. By the time he turned around again, the blanket folded haphazardly over his arm, she was wearing her shorts, blouse and sandals. Except for the salty tang that had replaced her perfume, she looked as if she'd never been near the water.

He picked up the ice chest and waited until she'd hooked the tote straps over her shoulder, then started toward the parking lot. He hadn't gone more than a half-dozen steps, though, before he realized that she wasn't coming along. She remained where she was, hands gripping the webbed straps tightly, staring out toward the water. He paused, shifted the ice chest to his other hand and waited a few moments more before speaking. "Hey."

Her muscles tightened, then relaxed as she turned. Though she was smiling, the look in her eyes was wistful. She was reluctant to leave, to return to town, where Taylor was only a few miles away, where his thugs were even closer.

Of course, she thought *he* was one of Taylor's thugs.

She caught up with him, and they trudged through the sand to the Mustang. She hadn't been talkative through dinner, and it was easy to continue not to talk as they drove back into town. No speeding this time, though the road ran straight and true and the state troopers rarely patrolled it.

He wasn't in a hurry to get where they were going.

Still, by the time it was fully dark they were

turning into the Sand Dollar parking lot. He slowed to little more than a crawl to cross the first speed bump, then the second. His headlights flickered across the back parking lot, glinting on a vehicle illegally parked in front of their apartments.

It was a silver Hummer.

"Taylor's here." Reaching into the glove compartment, Mitch pulled out an Atlanta Braves baseball cap and clamped it onto Jennifer's head. He made a sharp left onto the row of parking spaces next to the swimming pool, then headed back to the street.

Without protest, she tugged the hat lower over her face and slumped in the seat. Even when they'd put several blocks between them and the apartments, she kept her right hand up to block her face. "What do we do now?" she asked. "Drive around until he gives up and goes home?"

Ignoring the feeling of significance that accompanied her use of the word *we,* he frowned. "Have you ever known Taylor to give up?"

She frowned, too.

"Are you skittish about the dark?"

"Not particularly." Then she added, "I guess. I don't really spend much time outside after dark. Why?"

He turned right at the next street. "I'm going to drop you off a couple blocks on the other side of the park. When you get home, tell Taylor you went for a walk. If he asks how long you've been gone, don't tell him, because we don't know how long he's been waiting."

The look she gave him was haughty. "I didn't notice what time I left. Now that I live alone, I don't have to stick to somebody else's schedule."

"Good." Taylor did like his schedules. Even when they were kids, he'd had certain routines that he followed religiously, and anyone who'd wanted to hang out with him had done so, too. Obviously it had applied to his wife, as well.

The street they were on led into one of Belmar's oldest neighborhoods. The houses were a decent size, the yards big, the trees old and huge. Sidewalks ran parallel to the street, buckled in places where live oak roots had worked their way through, and bikes and toys littered the yards. During daylight hours there was always someone outside—playing, working in the garden, sitting on the porch—but tonight the street was quiet.

He pulled to the curb two blocks due east of the park and cut the headlights. Jennifer got out, then leaned into the backseat to get the tote.

"Leave that," he said. "Taylor's never going to believe you've gone for a long walk hauling that."

She nodded, dug out her keys and cell phone, then set the bag down again. "I go to the end of the block here and turn right?"

"Yeah."

She glanced down the street. If she was leery, it didn't show.

"I'll be around," he said anyway. If that would make her feel safer.

With another nod, she took a few steps away, then came back and dropped the baseball cap into the passenger seat. Running her fingers through her hair, she walked away again.

Mitch watched until she turned the corner, then he climbed out and moved the tote bag, blanket and ice chest to the trunk. What the hell was he doing helping Taylor's wife lie to him?

Protecting his own hide. Taylor didn't trust easily—a man in his position never did. If he thought for a minute that he couldn't trust Mitch, he'd fire his ass. And now, when Taylor had just offered misappropriated money, wasn't a good time to get fired. Not only would Mitch have wasted the last two months, but somebody else would be moving in on Jennifer. Somebody who didn't give a damn about her best interests where they conflicted with the boss's.

Sliding behind the wheel again, he drove slowly to the corner. Jennifer's white shirt reflected light from the streetlamp at the end of the block. Her pace was unhurried, her arms swinging to match. She was in no rush to get home and face her husband.

Estranged husband, Mitch irritably corrected.

He watched until she disappeared into the darkness underneath a canopy of broad trees that shadowed the street and the yards on both sides. Slowly he turned the corner, following at a distance without headlights. The city park was ahead, two blocks wide and three blocks long. By the time he reached it, she was strolling across the open grassy area where kids played soccer and baseball during the day. She was the only person out there tonight.

He pulled into the small parking lot that fronted the picnic pavilion and watched. A drainage ditch bordered the far side of the field. She hesitated along the edge, then found her way down, across and up again. From there it was less than fifteen feet across cropped grass to the apartment parking lot. To Taylor.

She cut far to the right of the Hummer but stopped when Taylor circled around the front of the vehicle. Jaw clenched, Mitch backed out of the space, drove onto the street, then headed for home. At the end of the park, he turned his headlights on again.

It took him little more than a minute to get home. Jennifer and Taylor were still standing next to the Hummer, ten feet separating them. Her arms were folded over her chest, her posture unfriendly, but she didn't appear distressed. Taylor was leaning against the Hummer's front fender, going for a casual look and not quite pulling it off.

Mitch parked in his usual spot, shut off the engine, then reluctantly got out. "Taylor," he greeted.

"Hey, Bubba," Taylor replied before shifting so his back was to Mitch. The message was clear enough.

There was nothing Mitch wanted less than to spend time with Jennifer and Taylor together, so walking from the car to the apartment door was easy. But there wasn't much he liked less at the moment than the idea of Jennifer spending time with Taylor alone, so going inside was tough. So was closing and locking the door.

He turned on lights in the living room, added the television for good measure, then went into the dark bedroom and eased the curtains away from the window far enough to see. Hearing, too, would be even better, but a man had to settle for what he could have.

Mitch wasn't real fond of settling.

* * *

"You gonna tell me where you've been?"

Jessica resisted the urge to tell Taylor where he could go and flashed a sarcastic smile instead. "You gonna tell me why it's any of your business?" So far he'd stuck to unimportant pleasantries, greeting her with a smug smile and phony concern for her well-being that might have gone over okay with Jennifer but made Jessica want to smack him hard.

"You're my wife. Of course I'm interested in what you're doing."

"We're separated."

His gesture was dismissive. "That doesn't mean anything."

"It means I don't have to keep anyone, especially you, informed of my movements." Then she made a gesture of her own, a disdainful wave toward Mitch's apartment. "Not that you need that sort of information from me. Your watchdogs are reporting regularly to you, aren't they?"

He didn't deny it. Of course, the surveillance had been blatant from the start. He'd wanted her

to know she was under his microscope, wanted
to remind her that he held the power both in this
town and this relationship. But Jen held the
evidence that could strip that power from him. If
only she could remember where it was or Jessica
could find it.

"Since I'm sure Officer Mitch—" she loaded his
name with sarcasm that she didn't feel, a fact she
would worry about later "—will tell you, I went
for a walk this evening. I don't know what time I
left. I don't know what time it is now. No watch."
She held up her left wrist so he could see it was
bare. "I don't know exactly what route I took, but
he can tell you that, too, since he was following
me like a good little guard dog. Satisfied?"

His reply was a grunt of the sort that had driven
Jen crazy. *God gave us language skills for a
reason,* she had complained whenever she was
on the receiving end of such a response. *Either
say something or keep quiet.*

Then he changed the subject. "I hear you had
lunch with Starla today."

He'd heard it straight from Starla's injected hooker-red lips. But Jessica merely smiled. "I did."

"Did she tell you how worried we all were about you?"

"Several times. Especially you." She faked a sugary accent. "Why, it broke her heart watchin' you grieve."

His gaze narrowed. "Why didn't you get in touch with me from the hospital?"

She turned to stare across the park she'd just crossed. That little walk tonight had told her she *wasn't* skittish about the dark...as long as someone big and strong was keeping an eye on her. Knowing that she could scream and Mitch would come running had banished a lot of the gremlins that might have been there otherwise.

"I just wanted to be with my sister." She shot him an accusing look. "I hadn't seen her in too long." That had been his doing, but if he felt guilty about it, it didn't show.

"One damn phone call, Jennifer. Was that too much to ask?"

"At the time, yes. I was more concerned about

recuperating from my injuries and spending time with Jessica."

"Your injuries?"

Her stomach clenched. How could he sound so unconcerned? So innocent? "From the accident," she said, reminding him of the lie he'd created. "My car washed off the road at Timmons Bridge."

"Oh, yeah. You must have hit your head pretty hard."

"I did. I had the lump to prove it. I just don't remember."

"Which part?" He shifted, crossing one ankle over the other, and Jessica caught a whiff of perfume on the night air. *Bastard.* He'd been with a woman before coming to see his wife.

"Any of it from the time I left the apartment. I remember rain, wind…and then I woke up in a hospital bed."

For a long time he studied her, no doubt deciding whether he believed her. If he did, wonderful. Maybe he'd pull off the guards and she would be free to get on with business. If he didn't, she would manage in spite of him.

"Why did you wait so long to try to evacuate? I told you to leave the day before. You couldn't take good advice just because it came from me?"

She shrugged negligently. In truth, that was part of the reason Jen had delayed. He was always giving orders, but that was one time she hadn't had to obey. Childish, yes, risking her safety to spite him, but satisfying, too. Then, as the storm had drawn closer to shore, she'd realized how busy he and his men were, overseeing the evacuation, helping business owners board up their places, protecting and serving the people in general, and she'd known she would never have a better chance to search for evidence of the crimes she had suspected him of committing. If she found it, she'd reasoned, she would evacuate it and herself all the way back to California, where she would turn it over to the proper authorities.

"I waited because I could," she said at last, head up, spine straight. "You couldn't make me go."

Again he studied her, reminding her of that microscope. "This isn't like you, Jennifer. When did you get so—"

"Bold?"

"Selfish. Who put these ideas in your head? That sister of yours? Jerri, Jacki, whatever the hell her name is?"

Jessica stared at him. "We were married three years. She was my only close family, and you never bothered to learn her name. You never met her, never let her visit, never let me go visit her. And you call me selfish." She walked away a few feet, then turned back. "Her name is Jessica. And, no, I didn't need her to put ideas in my head, Taylor. I'm not some empty-headed plastic doll like Starla who needs a man to tell her what to do and what to say. I'm fully capable of acting on my own."

He pushed away from the Hummer as she dug in her pocket for her keys. When she stepped onto the curb, he called from the middle of the parking lot. "This isn't over, Jennifer. Not until I get what I want."

She acknowledged his remark with nothing more than a scathing look before letting herself into the apartment. The locks clicked as she secured them, then she sagged against the solid weight of the door. "Bring it on, bastard," she murmured.

The hell with what he wanted. She was going to see to it that he got exactly what he deserved.

Seconds ticked past as she waited for the powerful engine of the Hummer to rev. Instead the only sound that came was a solid knock next door, followed by a rumble of voices. He'd gone to Mitch's apartment, no doubt to verify her story about the walk.

Maybe to find out if she'd bought Mitch's claim that he wasn't being a hundred percent truthful with Taylor? Was Mitch really less than committed to Taylor's spying program or had that merely been a ploy to gain her trust? Could he be that good an actor? Could she be that gullible?

Her cell phone beeped and she fished it from her pocket. Jennifer's sweet smiling face on the screen answered the last question for her: hell, yes, she could be that gullible. Look at Jen and how she'd fallen hook, line and sinker for Taylor's act. Maybe susceptibility to the wrong guy was just one more thing they shared in common.

Heaving a sigh, she flipped open the phone, then dropped onto the sofa. "I wish we could talk in person."

Jen laughed. "That's what passes for a greeting with you? We are talking in person."

"You know what I mean. Face-to-face."

"Yeah, well, that's not possible."

And hadn't been for a long time. No matter how much she would like to blame it on Taylor, Jessica had to accept some of the fault, and so did Jen. True, he had at first discouraged Jen from visits home, then flat-out denied her, and every time she'd suggested that Jessica come to Belmar, he'd always had an excuse for why it wasn't a good time. But they were both adults, capable of making airline and hotel reservations, paying for them, traveling on their own. They could have ignored Taylor's objections and gotten together anyway, in Belmar, Hong Kong or anyplace in between, but they'd chosen not to.

"I don't suppose you have any wonderful news for me," Jessica said, "such as 'You're looking for a flash drive and it's hidden in a shoe box in my closet.'"

"Nothing that wonderful, but I do remember something. I'm just not sure how much help it'll be."

Hope flared to life, warming Jessica from the inside out. "What is it?"

"Don." Hastily Jen went on. "I know. It's just a name. I don't think I know a Don there. It may not even have anything to do with Taylor or that night, but I have this feeling...."

Nothing wonderful was a major understatement. "Hey, it's something," Jessica said, trying to sound more optimistic than she felt. "I'll see what I can find out."

"Yeah, well, I hope it's not a dead end. Have you been to the house yet?"

"I haven't escaped the goon squad long enough yet. But I did have lunch with Starla." They traded a few jabs at the woman, reminding Jessica of old times. Cataloging other girls' clothing, makeup, hair and flaws had been a favorite pastime when they were younger. There had been a certain safety there. They could be as catty and petty as they wanted, knowing they would never hold it against each other.

"And what did you do for dinner?" Jen asked after a good laugh.

Jessica's fingers tightened around the small phone. She didn't want to answer the question, because *what* would lead to *where* and *with whom,* which would get her nothing but warnings. Still, she took a breath and said, "I had a picnic at Posey's Park."

"I lived in that town three years and you've been there two days and have already discovered places I didn't know existed. Where is that?"

"It's a beach a few miles east of town."

"How did you find it?"

The lump in Jessica's throat made swallowing difficult. "Just driving."

"Oh, Jess, you shouldn't go off to isolated places by yourself."

"I have a police escort everywhere I go, remember? I was safe." Or at least fooled into thinking so.

"Safe from others, maybe," Jen said quietly. "But who's going to keep you safe from *them?*"

Jessica knew too well how valid Jen's concern was. Still, she forced confidence she didn't feel into her voice. "I'm careful, Jen. I'm not taking unnecessary risks."

Liar! Spending any time at all with Mitch was unnecessary. Talking to him, looking at him, thinking that maybe she could trust him—those were all risks, if not to her life, then to her heart. She had no intention of losing either one.

"Of course you're taking risks, just by being there. I never should have asked you to do this. We should forget it, Jess. You should pack up and go home."

Taylor's last words echoed in Jessica's mind. *This isn't over, Jennifer. Not until I get what I want.* He'd gotten what he wanted his whole damn life, and at tremendous cost to those who got in his way. No more. It was time he paid.

"No. Don't worry, Jen. With your help, I can handle this. We can't just give up. Not now." Not when she'd met Taylor and seen for herself how arrogant and smug he was. Not when she believed she could succeed if she just had a fair chance. "It's only been a couple days. You didn't think I could waltz in, find the evidence and be gone again that quick, did you?"

After a moment's pause, Jen sheepishly admitted, "Well, you do negotiate multimillion-dollar contracts for breakfast."

"I don't negotiate. We have lawyers for that. I facilitate." She fell back on one of their mother's favorite sayings. "Rome wasn't built in a day, you know." And Taylor Burton, guilty of intimidation, extortion and who knew what else, wouldn't be destroyed in a day.

But it *would* happen.

"Just be careful, Jess."

"I will. Cross my heart." Immediately she winced. Bad choice of words. *Cross my heart, hope to die.* No way. She fully intended to live. "Call me if you remember anything else, okay?"

"I will."

As Jessica flipped the phone shut, Jen's whisper seemed to hang in the air. "Be *really* careful, Jess."

Chapter 6

Don. Sheesh, why couldn't Jen's lone memory been more substantial? If it had to have been a name, couldn't it have been a little less common? Mariah, Horace, Clementine. But Don?

Jessica lay on her stomach across the bed and ran through her personal list of Dons. Don Henley—great music. Don Knotts—had always made her father laugh. Donald Duck—had always made *her* laugh. Donald Trump—bad hair. *Don we now our gay apparel* and "Delta Dawn," two songs she didn't much care for.

This was ridiculous. The name must be significant to Belmar—someone Jen had known. In the morning she would go to the library and search the newspaper archives. Now she might as well get some sleep and—

A quiet rap made her entire body go still. It was ten o'clock at night; she would be wary of any visitor that late. But this knock hadn't been at the living room door. It had come at the metal door that connected one old motel room to the next— that connected her bedroom to Mitch's.

Warmth flooded through her as she stood. After talking with Jen, she'd showered and dressed for bed, forgoing her sister's matronly nightgowns for her own silk chemise. It was deep purple and fell halfway down her thighs—at least as modest as the clothing she'd worn earlier. Still, she couldn't resist wishing she'd brought the matching robe as she took the few steps to reach the door.

Her hand hovered over the lock, her fingers trembling. For heaven's sake, she chided herself. It was just a door, just Mitch wanting to return the things she'd left in his car.

Just a door that opened into his bedroom. And she was wearing a chemise—not called "intimate apparel" for nothing. And Mitch could never be "just" Mitch.

"Hey." His voice came through the door, low, strong, too sexy. "I've got your stuff."

She twisted the lock, undid the security latch and opened the door. He stood there, still in the shorts and shirt he'd worn to the beach, hair ruffled as if he'd dragged his fingers through it, beard stubbling his jaw. Big and strong...and handsomer than he had any right being. Than she had any right thinking about.

He set the tote and the ice chest on the floor beside her, then laid the blanket on top. For that instant, he was too close, and heat seeped through her pores at the same time goose bumps rose on her skin. Because his bedroom was cooler than hers, she reasoned, then frowned. She could lie to Taylor, to Mitch, even to Jen, but she wasn't in the habit of lying to herself. The air had nothing to do with it. It was all Mitch.

When he straightened, he looked at her—really looked, his gaze starting at her bare feet and working its way up to her face. His eyes darkened and a muscle in his jaw clenched. On another man, she might have mistaken his reaction for anger, but he wasn't any other man and he most definitely wasn't angry.

She shifted awkwardly, then hugged her arms to her middle. That pulled the silk tight across her breasts—she saw that when his gaze dropped—so she lowered her arms to her sides again. "Th-thanks for bringing my—my—" Dumbly she gestured, then fortified herself with a breath. "Did Taylor confirm my story with you?"

He nodded. "He also asked if I knew you claimed not to remember what happened that night. Is that true?"

She smiled thinly. "I don't remember a thing about an accident." How true was that? But then, there had been nothing accidental about what had happened to Jen that night. Taylor had meant to hurt her, to destroy her to save himself.

Still looking tense, Mitch leaned against the

doorjamb, one hand level with her face. Strong, long fingers. Her very first clue that Taylor wasn't what he seemed, Jen had said, only half teasing, was the fact that his nails were manicured. Mitch's weren't. They were cut very short, square, with a ragged cuticle on his index finger. They were nice hands. Capable. "I'm the one who saw you leaving the apartment that night. I told you it was too late to leave town and to go to the community center. You said you would, got in the car and drove away."

She took a step back and found the support of the door. Resting against it, she forced her attention to the conversation. "And soon after that I was swimming at Timmons Bridge."

"Why?"

"Because my car went off the road there?"

"Timmons Bridge isn't on the way out of town. It's not on the way anywhere."

Since she didn't know exactly where it was, she couldn't respond to that. She could only assume Taylor had chosen to dump Jen's car there because it had been convenient. That way, if her body was never found, everyone would believe it had washed away in the hurricane.

Deliberately she changed the subject, looking past him into the bedroom. "It doesn't look as if you've really moved in. Waiting for a house to come up for sale in Taylor's neighborhood before you unpack?"

He took a long look around her own room that seemed more intimate than it should. After all, other than the gown on her back, none of the belongings there were hers. "Waiting for Taylor to accept your terms so you can move back into his house before you unpack?"

"Not in this lifetime," she replied with a fake smile.

"Me either."

Damn it, she wanted to believe him.

In search of a distraction, she picked up the coverlet, gave it a shake, perfuming the air with the scents of sun and sand, then tossed it over the bed. "Why do you work for Taylor?" she asked conversationally as she straightened the edges.

"It's a nothing little job in a nothing little

town, and I wouldn't have even that if not for him. Remember?"

Color warmed her cheeks as she looked at him from across the bed. "I shouldn't have said that. Did you want to come home to Belmar?"

"It's not my home anymore." He took a few steps into the room, stopping to gaze at the pictures on the wall. Most of them were of her, shots she'd sent over the too-many months she and Jen had been apart; the only picture of Jen, standing on the deck of the cruise ship, could easily be mistaken for Jessica. It probably wasn't the first time Mitch had seen the pictures—he had almost surely been among those who'd searched the apartment after the hurricane—but he studied them as if it were.

"You've been to China."

Her hands stilled in smoothing wrinkles from the comforter. Jen's cruise was the only time she'd ever been out of the country. Did Taylor know that? Probably not. He hadn't remembered Jessica's name when she was sure Jen had mentioned her dozens of times—and she liked to think she was more important to her sister than past vacations.

"Wow, you figured that out from nothing more than a picture of me standing on the Great Wall," she said at last, moving to stand near enough to see the picture, not near enough to feel at risk. "Maybe you should be a cop."

"Funny." Instead of sarcastic, his voice was dry. "Maybe you should be a comedian."

Mitch looked at her from the corner of his eye, making an effort to not let his gaze slip lower than her chin. That little purple thing she was wearing, while covering everything that needed to be covered and then some, was still somehow tempting. Maybe because he knew she wasn't wearing anything under it. The tiny straps bared her shoulders and the fabric skimmed her hips too closely to conceal a thing. Or maybe because something like that was made for putting on only so it could be taken off.

Maybe because he would find damn near anything she wore tempting in his current state of mind.

His sidelong view of her was unfocused—hazy blond, golden, purple. There was nothing hazy about her scent, though. It was clean, simple, spicy, a far cry from the perfume she'd worn other times. This fragrance was shampoo, soap, lotion or some combination—all things he didn't need to be thinking about when he was standing two feet away from her with a bed only a few steps behind them.

Shifting his gaze forward, he looked at the picture again. Her clothes were similar to what she'd worn to the beach—khaki shorts, white shirt—but these shorts had little in common with those. These were at least eight inches shorter, revealing as much thigh as her swimsuit had, and the shirt was a tank top that fitted as if it were a size too small and revealed more than her swimsuit. Thick white socks were scrunched down at the tops of hiking boots that made a clunky contrast to her slender, muscular calves.

"My sister lived in Hong Kong for a while. One summer, after school was out, I went to visit. We walked the Great Wall for miles, just my guide and me. It was impressive."

"Jessica didn't go?"

She blinked, surprise flashing through her eyes, then shook her head. Surprised that he remembered her sister's name? Why wouldn't he? He'd gotten the car rental information; Jennifer had mentioned her.

"She was working."

"You traveled halfway around the world to see her and she worked?" He kept his tone mild, but she frowned at him anyway. She didn't like even vaguely implied criticism of her sister. He understood that. He could say what he wanted about his brothers, but when someone else criticized them, he took it very personally.

He glanced at the other pictures—Jennifer on a crowded beach, at the top of some mountain, outside what appeared to be a Buddhist temple. There were two shots of an older couple, both tanned and white-haired, the woman's features bearing a strong resemblance to Jennifer's. There were no pictures of Jessica. None of Taylor.

"Those are my parents," she said quietly, reaching out a pink-tipped finger to touch one frame. "They died eight months apart. Mom of cancer, Dad of a broken heart."

"You look like her."

She smiled, and he thought it might have been the first truly pleased smile he'd gotten from her in two days. "I know."

Abruptly she moved away, going to gaze out the window. To put plenty of space between them, he suspected. After a moment, she looked back. "Taylor had been with a woman before he came over here tonight."

Mitch knew that. Taylor hadn't said so outright, but he'd hinted at it, dropping Megan's name along with a wink and a grin. Had he thought Jennifer was too clueless to notice or that she wouldn't care? Or had *he* just not cared? "Sorry."

She made a dismissive sound, accompanied by a shrug that made her gown ripple over her skin. It made something ripple over his skin, too. Heat. Hunger. Insanity. She was married, and he didn't fool around with married women. Period.

Never had, never would. No matter how tempting she was.

"Fidelity doesn't mean much to most guys," she said casually.

"It does if they've been raised right or if they've seen what infidelity can do." He'd already told her he was illegitimate, something few people currently in his life knew. With a shrug, he offered up a few more private details. "My mother had been engaged to my father for almost a year when she got pregnant. That was when she found out that he was already married and that she wasn't the only woman he was seeing on the side. It hurt her, hurt his wife, hurt his kids, all because he wouldn't keep his pants zipped."

"Most people say 'couldn't.'"

This time the derisive sound was his. He would have sworn, but the appropriate curse was one he didn't use in front of women. Another result of having been raised right. "People who sleep around do it because they want to, not because they're compelled to. They do it because they're selfish and they don't give a damn about anyone but themselves. Their marriage vows mean nothing to them. Betraying this person they've sworn to be faithful to means nothing. They don't—"

She was looking at him strangely, her mouth almost curved into a smile, her gaze steady and intense. He realized he was about as close to ranting as he ever got and drew a breath. "Being called Charlotte Lassiter's or Gerald Calloway's bastard even once was one time too many for me. Sorry."

"Don't be. People should feel passionate about something, and living by vows made before God isn't a bad choice."

He felt passionate about more than that. Did she know she could tempt him? Did she have a clue that he'd thought about her alone in his bed last night? Did she have any idea that he could want her almost enough to forget that she was married? *Almost.*

She folded her arms beneath her breasts again, pulling the fabric taut. Even from this distance, he could see her nipples pressed hard against the material. Because it was cool in the room? Or because he wasn't the only one tempted?

She looked out of place there—too pretty, too elegant for badly textured wallboard, cheap carpet and tacky curtains. But she didn't seem to notice. She didn't act as if she were slumming, even though Taylor boasted how very particular she was about being surrounded by the best.

She was watching him with the look he'd come to associate with serious discussion, her expression as bland as her gaze was intense. "Are you really not telling Taylor everything?"

He mimicked her position against the connecting door and shook his head.

"Why not?"

How much to tell her? How much would she believe? Truth: he didn't like being used. Didn't like keeping watch on someone who wasn't a suspect in a crime. Didn't believe it was any of Taylor's business how Jennifer spent her time. Didn't think Taylor should use city resources for his personal gain, especially when Mitch *was* those resources.

"He warned me," he said at last.

"About what?"

"That there would be consequences if I did anything more than watch you."

"And you believe that would be a bad thing."

Oh, hell, yeah, he believed it. But his only response was a shrug, and that was enough for her. For a moment she just looked at him. Her breathing was slow and steady, her lips parted just a bit, the pulse at the base of her throat a barely visible throb. She looked stronger and more capable than he'd thought the prehurricane Jennifer capable of and she attracted him in ways the prehurricane Jennifer couldn't have. She made him want to push away from the door, walk around the bed, close those last few feet between them and touch her.

Just touch. Feel how warm and soft and smooth she was. Compare the texture of golden skin to nicely developed muscle. Measure the beat of her heart with his fingertips. Feel the soft rise and fall of her chest. Touch her. With his fingers and his hands and his mouth and his body.

He swallowed hard, hot and too damn close to getting hard, and she yawned. It wasn't a delicate little yawn that she could hide behind one hand but bigger, screwing up her whole face, then making her grin.

"Sorry. My mom used to say I was like the Energizer bunny. I go and go and go, and when I stop, I shut down completely."

He almost managed a wry smile, but frustration kept it from forming completely. "I'll go." He'd taken a step toward his own apartment when she spoke again.

"Hey. Don't think I didn't notice that you avoided my question earlier."

"What question was that?"

"Why do you work for Taylor?"

Not because it was my choice. But that wasn't true. He could have gone somewhere else, done something else. There was one reason why he hadn't, and he gave it to her. "I'm a cop. This is what I do."

"You could have been a cop someplace else."

"I needed to do it here."

If the answer didn't satisfy her, she didn't let it show. Instead she moved to fold down the covers on the bed. The sheets were striped, white on white, and looked a hell of a lot more expensive than the set he'd picked up at Wal-Mart on his way to Belmar.

"Can I ask one more question?"

"If I say no, you're going to ask anyway, aren't you?"

She smiled briefly, smugly. "Do you know anyone in town named Don?"

He didn't know what he'd expected, but that wasn't it. He blinked before shrugging. "Don Miller owns the abstract office downtown. Donny Dominguez is the high school football coach. Don Scott runs the Chevy dealership, and Donald Field is on staff at the hospital. I'm sure there are more, but those are the ones I know. Why?"

"I don't know." She shook her head, her hair swaying gently. "The name's been in my head and I can't figure out why."

Not likely. But he couldn't accuse her of lying. Well, actually, he could and, if necessary, would, but tonight it wasn't necessary. Instead he walked through the open doorway into his own room, then turned back. "I'll see you tomorrow."

"Of course you will." She closed and locked the door.

A moment later, he did the same with his own door.

The John J. Belmar Public Library was located on a quiet side street a few blocks from downtown with a church across the street and the town's residential area starting on its east side. It was an impressive building, constructed of great blocks of stone brought in, no doubt, at great expense. Ole John J. apparently hadn't been satisfied naming both town and library after himself but had wanted the building to be worthy of that name.

Jessica parked on the street beside a magnolia and headed for the main entrance. She couldn't remember the last time she'd been in a library, probably sometime in high school. With laptop computers and the Internet, she'd never found the need since then. But walking inside resurrected the feelings from years ago, when her mother had taken her and Jen to their local library on a regular basis. It was the stillness, the high ceilings, the marble floors, the shelves and shelves of books, the feeling that this was a special place deserving of respect.

It was a place creepy Jimmy Ray clearly had no use for, evidenced by the disdain on his face when he came through the doors a few moments behind her. She wandered through the stacks, mostly to annoy him, occasionally picking up a book, then returning it to the shelf. He made no effort to hide the fact that he was following—at least until a young woman seated at one of the tables caught his attention. The moment he sat down across from her, Jessica headed for the newspapers-and-periodicals section.

The Belmar newspaper wasn't available online, the librarian told her, but she was happy to direct her to stacks of papers and rolls of microfilm. She could look for information the old-fashioned way, Jessica thought with a half smile, half grimace, before approaching the shelves. If she at least had a clue what she was looking for, it wouldn't seem so daunting a task. But reading months' worth of a small-town newspaper looking for a mention of someone named Don who might or might not be pertinent to Jen…

She gave a soft sigh. What else did she have to do with the kid cop dogging her steps?

She started with the top twelve inches of neatly stacked newspapers. It was published every day but Saturday and ran sixteen pages, with news and classifieds in the front section and society and sports in the back, plus advertising inserts on Wednesday and Sunday. It was the sort of paper that included details of four-year-olds' birthday parties, write-ups of Little League games and pictures of lost pets. If you wanted in-depth national or international news, you had to look elsewhere, but if you wanted to know who got arrested, who was getting married or divorced or which bowling team led the league, the *Herald* was your paper.

Her impatience—and her certainty that she

was indulging in a wild-goose chase—faded as she read. If she overlooked the frequent mentions and photographs of Taylor, the paper was really quite charming. The staff could use a refresher course in spelling and grammar, but at least their hearts were in their work. They were as enthusiastic about the latest yard-of-the-week winner as they were about the most recent murder.

It had happened over three months ago and was still unsolved. The victim had been a teenage girl, blond and pretty and looking far more sophisticated than her sixteen years. The photo was a glamour shot, with the girl wearing something low and off the shoulders, her hair too styled, her makeup too heavy.

And her name was Tiffani Dawn Rogers.

"Catching up on what happened in town while you were gone?"

Jessica startled, barely curbing the impulse to sweep the newspaper under the table. Instead she folded it in half and laid it so the girl's picture wasn't visible before lifting her gaze to Mitch. He stood a few feet away, the latest issue of a sports magazine open in his hands, and looked for all the world as if he found its contents captivating.

Something tingled inside her, but it wasn't surprise. Hadn't she deliberately planned this trip for lunchtime in the hopes that Jimmy Ray would take a break to eat? And hadn't she figured, based on her limited experience, that if Jimmy Ray did take a break, Mitch would be the one to relieve him? As if she wasn't seeing enough of him at night.

Well, not really enough but more than she needed. Just not more than she wanted.

She glanced around, saw no one paying them any mind, then replied in a voice as quiet as his had been. "It seemed better than actually speaking to Taylor."

"You spoke to Taylor last night." It was a simple reminder. There was nothing important about it, nothing of substance, except for the underlying emotion. Not quite jealousy, not quite resentment, but close.

"Not my choice," she replied. "Someone threw me out of his car so I had no place to go but home."

He turned the magazine's page. "What would you have preferred?"

"I don't know. Maybe driving away like a bat out of hell and not coming back until he was gone."

"He would have waited." He flipped another page, then asked, "Aren't you hungry? For barbecue?"

Down Home, of course, and he would join her. Even if she hadn't been hungry before he'd asked, she was now. "Yeah, I think I am. Give me a minute." She pushed her chair back, the feet scraping on the floor earning a look from the librarian. Smiling apologetically, she reorganized the stack of papers, turned and saw the copy machine against the wall. She hesitated, then thumbed through, pulled out the Tiffani Dawn story and went to the machine.

It cost her a buck twenty-five to copy the story that filled most of two pages. Quickly she folded the copy in half and stuffed it in her purse, then put the papers away. Without glancing at Mitch, she headed for the door and outside into the warm day. By the time she reached her car, he was coming out the door. By the time she'd circled the block and turned north on Ocean, he was a few car lengths behind her.

She found her way to the restaurant without a problem. The parking lot was packed, all the tables along the three-sided porch filled with diners. Some of them watched curiously as she walked to the front of her car. When Mitch joined her, they returned to their conversations.

A pretty young woman greeted them inside the door, her hair intricately braided with beads that clacked when she rose onto her toes to hug Mitch. "I figured we'd see you today or tomorrow. After all, it's been a whole day and a half since you were here."

"Hey, Liana." When she stepped back, he nodded to Jessica. "This is Jennifer. Liana is Willis's oldest daughter."

The girl gave Jessica a long look that, despite its blandness, struck her as disapproving. When she smiled, though, it was enough to take a person's breath away. "Welcome to the best barbecue in the state of Mississippi. We have a table for two—"

Mitch interrupted. "How about the family table? Is it available?"

Liana looked from him to Jessica, then back again. "Sure. It's always available for you. This way."

The family table was out back, an old pedestal table that sat in the shade of a massive oak tree. Comfortable cane chairs circled it, their paint flaked, and a cool breeze drifted around it. A line of azaleas blocked their view of the parking lot, and the only visible part of the restaurant was the kitchen. An isolated table at an out-of-the-way restaurant. If that wasn't clandestine, Jessica didn't know what was.

Using the connecting doors to pass between apartments without being seen, a voice whispered slyly. *Using those doors to do more than just talk.*

Face flushing, she chose the chair nearest the tree trunk. She ordered iced tea and a pulled-pork sandwich. Mitch ordered the same, plus a side of ribs. After Liana disappeared inside the restaurant, Jessica remarked, "She's beautiful."

"Yeah. She looks like her mama, thank God."

It was her mother who had served them Wednesday night, who'd said, *Just make sure the fingers you lick are your own,* then given them a wicked smile. She'd been pretty, too, but not like her eldest daughter.

"What were you doing at the library?"

She didn't look at Mitch but gazed off into the woods behind the restaurant. The thick canopy of trees blocked the sun, leaving little undergrowth nearby. More distant, though, bushes, vines and saplings grew in a tangle. "I was annoying Jimmy Ray," she said at last. "A worthy way to spend a morning, don't you think?"

"Jimmy Ray's a punk," he said. "But he's a mean punk. Don't forget that."

"Starla thinks in a few years he might be God's gift to women."

"Not unless God has one hell of a warped sense of humor. I figure in a few years he'll be in prison or dead."

Her gaze jerked to him, but this time he was the one looking away. "And Taylor?" *Please, God, if I have anything to say about it.*

He didn't answer. Instead he leaned down, unzipped her purse where it rested near her feet and pulled out the photocopies she'd made.

"Hey!" She grabbed for them, but he caught her hand effortlessly with his free hand, and everything else faded. His touch was firm, his skin extraordinarily warm. He wasn't hurting her, though she knew he could—if his grandmother hadn't raised him right. No, pain—or getting free—was the last thing on her mind. Instead, she stared at those long brown fingers and imagined them stroking along the sensitive skin inside her wrist, making the pulse there thud double time...or slowing it down until it barely beat, lost in a lazy, hot, sensual haze that would rob her breath from her lungs and make her weak and needy and...

He released her hand, but she swore she could still feel his touch. Could feel it in places where he hadn't ever touched her.

Unaffected by the very brief moment, he stared at the bad black-and-white of Tiffani Dawn's picture, then his jaw tightened and a vein pulsed in his throat. "What's your interest in this?"

Her stomach knotted, and she had to think about how to swallow. Wishing Liana would hurry back with her tea, she tried for a casual shrug that was jerky. "Murder in a small town. I don't know much about it. Morbid curiosity."

"How could you not know much about it? Taylor was calling press conferences every other hour."

She gave another pathetic shrug. "I told you, I try not to talk to Taylor or to listen when he talks. Did they ever find the person responsible?"

His jaw tightened even more and his answer was clipped. "No."

"No suspects?"

"No."

The kitchen screen door banged, pulling his gaze that way. He folded the pages, creased them sharply with his thumb, then slid them under his thigh, out of sight, as Liana made her way toward them.

Assuming Mitch and Willis were Taylor's age, that would make Liana about seventeen. Had she known Tiffani Dawn? Been friends with her? Mourned her?

She served their drinks and food along with a tall carafe of iced tea, warned Mitch not to leave without saying hello to her parents, then returned to the restaurant. For a time they concentrated on eating. Jessica was dipping a piece of fried okra into ranch dressing when he broke the silence.

"The other night, it probably took you about two seconds to figure out that this is the wrong side of town. Tiffani Dawn Rogers grew up a half mile from here. She lived in a trailer house back in the woods. Her mother was a drunk, and her father was in and out of jail. She was in trouble from the time she learned to walk and talk— shoplifting, drinking, drugs, sex. She was the girl that all the guys slept with but didn't want to be seen in public with."

The okra was hot on Jessica's fingers. She set it down and wiped her hands.

"She ran around with older, wilder kids. This past May she went to a graduation party with some of them. The last anyone saw of her, she was driving away from the party at four in the morning. Her car was found three days later, parked on a dead-end street, and her body was in the trunk. There was evidence of sex with multiple partners, though no sign of force, and she had been choked."

The story—and his quiet, emotionless recitation—made Jessica's stomach queasy. Grateful she'd gotten most of her lunch down already, she pushed the plate away. "You weren't here then."

"No. I came about a month later."

"And Taylor the hotshot police chief hasn't solved the case." Dear God, because he was somehow involved in it? Was that why the name meant something to Jen?

Mitch looked at her, his dark eyes bleak, his mouth a taut line. "It's one of the sorry truths in this country that there's no such thing as 'justice for all.' Tiffani Dawn was trash. She lived in the wrong place, had the wrong parents, the wrong background. Her behavior likely contributed to her death. If she'd been the mayor's daughter or the city manager's or the state senator's, solving her murder would have been a top priority. But she wasn't and it wasn't."

"And that's Taylor's fault." Jessica couldn't understand how her sister had fallen for such a selfish, egotistical and heartless son of a bitch. He was so obviously wrong for her—wrong for any woman with a smidgen of humanity. How had it happened and why had it taken so long for her to open her eyes?

He was so very good at pretending, and I was so very much in love.

Poor Jen, believing the man was deserving of love or capable of giving it. She'd learned her lesson but not without great cost.

"So her body was found and Taylor did what?"

"Processed the car. She wasn't killed there, though, and they never found the crime scene. They conducted what looked like a competent investigation, but after the initial media coverage— after all, she was a pretty teenage girl—everyone lost interest, including the department."

"Have you looked into it?"

He gave her a long, level look. "Why do you ask?"

Because it was something the cop she wanted

him to be would do. Because Tiffani Dawn hadn't deserved to die and certainly not that way. Because it was the right thing to do.

She didn't tell him any of that, though. "Just curious."

"You're curious about all sorts of things today, aren't you?"

"Does her mother still live here?"

"No. She moved to Georgia not long after the funeral. By then, the reporters had stopped calling and the detectives had turned their attention to other cases."

"And when you came, you read the reports. You were curious, too."

"I'm a cop. It's what I do."

She leaned back in her chair, holding her glass in one hand. It was a warm day, too warm to be comfortable outside without the breeze and the shade. The heat and the cool caress of air across her skin made her lethargic, lazy…though not a sleepy sort of lazy. She was too aware—of Mitch, of herself. Her limbs felt heavy, and her skin seemed to hum with tension. Her nipples ached, and long-unsatisfied desire curled, wispy and faint, in her belly.

Sitting here near the man, looking at him, listening to his voice, was turning her on. God, was she as gullible as Jen?

"You don't give straight answers very often, do you?" she asked as he finished his lunch, then cleaned his hands. *Make sure the fingers you lick...* With a sudden rush of heat flaring inside her, she drained the tea in her glass, leaving nothing but ice cubes and a few amber drops.

"I haven't told you anything that isn't true," he replied, picking up the carafe, silently offering a refill before adding, "in one way or another."

She extended her glass and he filled it to the brim. "It's the 'one way or another' that worries me."

"And you've been a hundred percent honest and forthcoming with me."

Of course she hadn't. He believed she was her sister. That pretty much made everything else about her suspect. But she'd been as honest as she could in her lies—easier to remember them—

and she was being dishonest for a good cause. What was his cause? Keeping illegal money flowing into his bank account without disruption? Protecting his crooked boss? Looking out for himself? None of that began to compare to making certain Taylor paid for his crimes.

And if Taylor was arrested, Mitch probably would be, too. The realization left her faintly nauseous.

"When it takes you that long to consider whether you've been honest, it's not a good sign."

She glanced at Mitch, who was *this* close to smiling. "Sorry. I was thinking about something."

"I could see that." He glanced at his watch, then shifted to pull his wallet from his hip pocket. The photocopy of the news story fluttered to the ground, and she retrieved it, returning it to her purse.

"I'll make you a deal," he offered as he removed a twenty. "You can ask me one question, any question, and I'll answer it truthfully. Then I get to ask you one, and you'll do the same."

"How can I know you're being truthful?"

He raised one hand. "I swear on my grand-mother's life."

"Your grandmother's dead."

"But her life meant one hell of a lot. I would never dishonor her by lying."

It was so very tempting, and she had some ideas for her question. *Can I trust you? Are you dirty? Are you the sort of man who would make your grandmother proud?* But she had a pretty good idea what his question would be, as well. *What are you up to?* He'd asked it before in various forms and he'd never been satisfied with her answers.

With a wary smile, she shook her head. "No deal."

"And you say I have a problem with straight answers." Sliding his chair back, he got to his feet, drained the last of his tea, then gestured toward the restaurant. "You want to come in while I say hello to Willis?"

Jessica thought of the look Willis had given her Tuesday night when he'd heard the Burton name and the similar look from Liana when they'd arrived and shook her head. "I'll go on to the car."

"Don't leave without me," he warned, and she gave him a dry look.

"As if I'd get far."

"Remember that," he said with a grin that damn near buckled her knees.

She watched him cross the grass with long, easy strides, take the steps two at a time, then go inside the kitchen. Finally she took a breath, got her purse and started across the side yard to the parking lot. Two days ago she would have taken his last words as a threat. Today she would much rather think of them as a promise.

No doubt about it. She was every bit as gullible as Jen. The big question now: was Mitch as dangerous to her as Taylor had been to Jen?

And how could she find out before it was too late?

Chapter 7

"You have a death wish I don't know about?"

Leaning against the kitchen counter, Mitch watched Willis watch Jennifer walk to her car. When she was out of sight and his old friend turned to face him, his look was disbelieving.

"Do I need to remind you that she's married? And to Taylor Burton, of all people?"

"I haven't forgotten. Besides, it's not what you think."

Willis still stared. "I think you're meeting out here because it's guaranteed that you won't run into anyone who'd tattle to Burton. You telling me I'm wrong?"

Not about that—as far as it went. "Where's LaRae?" he asked instead of answering.

Willis looked out the window one more time. "She's gone to the bank. Lucky for you, too. Seeing you with Burton's wife again, she'd snatch you bald."

"They're separated."

"That ain't the same as divorced."

No, but neither of them seemed to have any interest in reconciling. That made it pretty close. It also made him wonder for the hundredth time exactly what they *were* interested in. Why had she come back? Why did Taylor have her under constant surveillance?

"Look, I know what I'm doing. Trust me." He gave his best, smuggest grin, the one that Lou could never decide whether to laugh at or slap away. She had usually ended up laughing.

Shaking his head, Willis rolled his eyes heavenward. "You hear that, Miz Lou? He knows what he's doing. He says I should trust him."

In a testament to coincidence—or God's and Lou's senses of humor—a clap of thunder shook the old house. Mitch laughed at the timing, then slapped Willis on the shoulder. "Tell LaRae I'm sorry I missed her. See you around."

"Yeah, yeah. And I guess we be seeing her, too."

Mitch left the kitchen and tracked down Liana at the register. She chattered while ringing up the bill and making change, and he responded absently.

"Sheesh," she said huffily, dropping a few bills into his hand. "I know when I'm being ignored. You sound just like Daddy."

"Sorry, hon. I've just got things on my mind." He gave the change back to her for a tip.

"Yeah." The beads in her hair clicked as she shook her head vigorously. "I saw what you have on your mind—or should I say who. Can I give you a piece of advice?"

He straightened his shoulders and gazed down at her. She was six inches shorter, slender as a reed and looked about as young and innocent as they came. "How old are you, Liana?"

"Seventeen."

"Young enough to be my daughter. You know, this may come as a surprise to you, but I have known a few women in my life."

A broad grin split her face, reminding him of Jennifer's comment. *She's beautiful.* She certainly was, and he was damn glad he was nothing more than her surrogate uncle. If he'd been Willis, he would have locked her away in the attic long before now to keep her safe.

Locking Jennifer away, out of Taylor's reach, was a pretty damn appealing idea.

"But you're a man, Mitch. Men just don't get it when it comes to women."

He tweaked one of her braids. "If you're speaking from experience, I don't want to know. See you next time." He reached the door in a couple of steps, then turned back. "Listen, about Jennifer…" It was a given that neither Willis nor LaRae would ever mention seeing her to anyone, but Liana was a kid.

Not too much of a kid, though. "Jennifer who?" she asked innocently, and if he hadn't known better, he would have believed her. She grinned again, this time with a wink. "See ya."

He went outside, stopping on the porch to put on his sunglasses. What was he doing asking a seventeen-year-old girl to cover for him? His job was tough enough as it was. He shouldn't be adding any behavior that needed covering.

If he had half a brain, he would demand Taylor take him off this surveillance…which would piss off the boss—never a good idea but in his circumstances a particularly bad one. Even if it didn't make Taylor angry and he did assign someone else, Mitch didn't *want* anyone else following Jennifer. He could trust himself. He couldn't say that about anyone else in the department.

So, since asking for an out wasn't an option, he should do what Taylor had told him to do— more or less. Keep an eye on her. Not go to dinner with her. Not picnic at the beach. Not stand in her bedroom talking. For damn sure not thinking about the better things they could have done in that bedroom that wouldn't have required the exchange of a single word.

Just keep an eye on her.

Yeah, right.

She was sitting in her car, windows down, music coming from the stereo. Her fingers were tapping on the steering wheel, spotlighted by the sun overhead, and he realized that she wasn't wearing any rings. The hunk-of-a-diamond engagement ring, the matching-but-smaller-hunks wedding ring, both gone…and nothing to show where they'd been. Not that she had much of a tan, but shouldn't three years of wearing rocks like those have left a mark?

His radio crackled as he walked behind her car to his patrol unit. Absently he answered.

"Where y'at?" Jimmy Ray asked.

"Headed west on Johnson Street." It would be true in another thirty seconds.

"Jeez, ain't nothin' out that way. I'll pick you up when you reach Ocean."

"Ten-four."

That was all of five minutes later. Jennifer turned left toward downtown and the Sand Dollar, and Jimmy Ray, driving one of the department's unmarked cars, pulled in behind her. Mitch turned around in a vacant parking lot and drove back the way he'd come.

The road leading to the Rogers home was an overgrown dirt lane, easy to miss if you didn't know it was there. Weeds brushed the sides of his car, and it bottomed out on the ruts a couple times before he reached the clearing.

A person could be forgiven for thinking the hurricane had done some damage to the place. In fact, it hadn't. Except for a little debris here and there, carried along by the water, it looked much the same as it had the first time Mitch had seen it. Shabby. Poor. A despairing place for a pretty little girl who'd wanted something more.

My baby shouldn't have died like that, Rhonda Rogers had sobbed.

She shouldn't have, Mitch agreed grimly. But she shouldn't have had to live like this, either. If Rhonda had just made a few different choices. If she had decided at some time in the past sixteen years that her daughter was more important than the drinking, the partying and the worthless husband who was gone more often than not. If she'd acted like a mother before it was too late.

He climbed out of his car and leaned against the fender, gazing at the gaping holes where window glass had once been. A tattered curtain fluttered in the breeze from what had been Tiffani Dawn's bedroom, and broken blinds dangled from a living room window.

Presumably Tiffani Dawn was the "Don" Jennifer had asked about the night before. Why? Had she really not remembered the first or last name? Had she been somehow testing him? And back to the original question: why?

He'd bet all of Taylor's illegal payoffs combined that Jennifer had never heard of Tiffani Dawn until her death. Wrong age group, wrong social circle for Police Chief Burton's wife. That made a test to check his reaction, to find out what he knew, unlikely.

He needed to find out what *she* knew and how she knew it. Did she suspect Taylor? Did she think he'd had more reasons than the

Rogerses' lack of social status for not conducting a real investigation?

A bird called from the high branches of a nearby pine, a mournful sound in a mournful place. Mitch got back into his car, drove to the nearest business—a down-on-its-luck liquor store—and dropped a few coins in the pay phone at its corner.

A woman answered Rick's cell phone, her voice husky as she called his brother's name. When he came on the line, Mitch greeted him with a snort. "Working hard, I see."

"Hey, even bartenders get time off now and then."

"Did you get the information I asked for?"

"Yeah." There was the sound of shuffling papers. "You wanted to know if Jennifer Burton could afford to bribe you. The answer is yes, unless you're the greediest son of a bitch that ever lived. She didn't make a whole lot when she was working—she was a schoolteacher—but when her parents died, she and her sister inherited a not-so-small fortune that sister has invested wisely."

"How not-so-small?"

Rick rattled off a figure that made Mitch whistle softly. "You think Taylor knew about it?"

"You think she'd still have it if he did?" Rick asked drily. "The big bucks are in her name only."

"She can buy and sell Taylor—and she's living in a cheap motel and driving a Chevy that's a rental." Didn't quite jibe with Taylor's description of her. But Mitch already knew that.

"Have you learned anything else about her?"

Plenty. Just not much that wouldn't get him a warning from Rick. After hearing it from Willis and again from Liana, he wasn't up for it a third time. "She asked me last night who around here was named Don, then went to the library this morning, pulled a bunch of old newspapers and copied the first story about Tiffani Dawn Rogers's murder."

"Why?" One word, but Rick managed to put a lot of suspicion into it.

"She said she was curious."

"You believe that's all it is?"

Remembering the deal he'd offered her after

lunch—one question each, one truthful answer—Mitch rubbed the ache settling in the back of his neck. "No."

After a moment, Rick went on. "You want to share with me what you do believe?"

He believed Jennifer was up to something. He knew it involved Taylor and suspected it was dangerous. Anything involving Taylor was. He also knew that Taylor was guilty of a lot of things. But was he capable of threatening his wife? Hurting her? Maybe even killing her?

Mitch had to assume he was. He had to keep her safe, which meant he had to get her to tell him what she knew.

"Mitch? You still there?"

"Yeah. Hell, Rick, I don't know what I believe." Thunder rumbled through the air as the sun disappeared behind heavy clouds, and the first raindrops splattered, fat and raising dust. "Listen, it's starting to rain here. I've got to go. I'll call you later."

"You be careful," Rick said in place of goodbye.

Mitch hung up, then dashed through the increasing rain to his car. Settled behind the wheel, he dug in the glove box for a napkin, then wiped the water from his face. He started the engine and flipped the air conditioner to high, then sighed.

How the hell was he going to persuade Jennifer to trust him?

After watching the rain for a time, Jessica turned on the television to the Weather Channel. A map of the gulf filled most of the screen, with a computer-generated funnel marking Hurricane Leonardo's current location. They were still predicting that it would make landfall on the Texas coast sometime in the next week, but their predictions, the meteorologist admitted, were nothing more than educated guesses. The slightest change in the storm's path could bring it ashore anyplace in the gulf.

Including Belmar.

Just what she needed. Taylor, Mitch *and* a hurricane.

Too restless to settle down, she wandered the apartment, studying photographs she knew by heart, looking in prospective hiding places that she'd already checked. She still didn't have a clue how to get into Taylor's house to search there, but there was one place left to search: Jen's storage unit in town. And what better time than a dreary, wet afternoon?

Jessica changed into shorts with neat creases and a pressed camp shirt—Jen's idea of casual— and grabbed a towel from the linen closet before shrugging into Jen's royal-blue slicker. She tucked the key to the locker in her pocket, kicked off her sandals and, with the shoes tucked beneath the slicker's cover, ran through ankle-deep water to the car.

The storage place was on the west side of town. A stack of soggy cardboard boxes, bearing the sign *We Sell Boxes,* stood next to the entrance. She drove through the gate and cruised slowly to the first locker in the third row. The kid cop hung back until she'd unlocked the door and stepped inside. Then he drove past, made a tight U-turn between units and parked twenty feet away, facing her.

The space wasn't large, maybe ten by twenty feet, and was lit by a single bare bulb overhead. The door lifted like a garage door; she pulled it down again after her. No need to let Jimmy Ray watch.

After shucking the slicker, she dried off with the towel and shoved her feet into the sandals. Then she took a long look around.

The space was seriously organized, no less than she would have expected from Jen. The furniture was old enough to have sentimental value but no antique value—pieces given to her by their parents and grandparents. The boxes were stacked according to size, and the contents were clearly marked: Childhood Souvenirs, College, Gifts from Students, Photographs. Jessica would have loved to find one labeled My Secret Evidence Against Taylor, but no such luck.

She searched the furniture first, taking cushions off the settee, removing drawers from the china buffet, dropping to the concrete floor to look underneath everything. She searched between the mattress and springs that leaned against one wall and in every cubby in an old wood cabinet. And she remembered—the settee in Jen's living room in Los Angeles, the family meals served on the buffet, the sleek side chairs they'd used to gain access to Grandma's cookie jar. They had argued over the cheval mirror that didn't match anything either of them owned but both of them wanted anyway. In the end, Jen had gotten it, but not without giving Jessica the oak dining table and six chairs.

By the time she finished with the furniture, she was hot and sweaty and a headache was forming from the overwhelmingly musty odors. If she kept the door closed, Jimmy Ray couldn't see what she was doing, but she wasn't going to last much longer without fresh air. Besides, what if he did see? What difference would his report make to Taylor? *She went through some boxes in the storage unit.* No big deal.

Taking hold of the metal lip that ran along the inside bottom of the door, she heaved it up, and the temperature in the space dropped by ten degrees. The rain still fell, steady but not torrential, smelling sweet and clean, clearing her lungs.

Jimmy Ray had left his car, taking shelter under the roof overhang across the way. He held a cell phone to his ear with one hand and a smoldering cigarette in the other. Passing on information to Taylor? Or taking advantage of his boring assignment to keep up with his social life? The idea that he even had a social life raised goose bumps on Jessica's arms, but Starla claimed he had potential.

Shutting him out of her thoughts, she turned to the boxes that stood four high along one wall. None of the labels held more promise than the others—Gifts from Students didn't seem likely to hold anything of more than sentimental value—but wasn't the unlikeliest hiding place the best? Taking that particular box from its stack, she set it on the floor, drew one of the side chairs near and peeled off the tape that secured the top.

The contents were exactly as marked—cards, trinkets, knickknacks and ornaments, most with apples. *I hate apples,* Jen had confided after her first year teaching. *I'd rather never have another gift than get another apple.* Naturally Jessica's next gift for her had been a blown-glass paper-weight in the shape of an apple. Jen had laughed—and saved all these apples.

Jessica had worked her way through several boxes, some of the items bringing back bitter-sweet memories, some unfamiliar to her, when the sound of an engine caught her attention. She looked up to see Jimmy Ray toss his cigarette into the water swirling toward the drain and straighten his thin shoulders an instant before Taylor's Hummer turned onto the lane. A chill ran up her spine. Talking to him last night, knowing Mitch was nearby, had been distasteful enough. Today, in the privacy of the storage unit, with no one around but Jimmy Ray…

She shuddered.

Taylor parked beside her car, blocking the way for any other traffic. He trotted around her car and into the unit and looked graceful doing it, with minimal splatter on his shirt. Even so, he took a moment to comb his palm over his hair, to straighten his cuffs and brush away a raindrop or two.

Seated two-thirds of the way to the back, Jessica fixed an unwelcoming look on him. "I didn't invite you inside."

"I'm the chief of police. I go where I want."

"Being chief doesn't make you God."

A grin brightened his face. "Almost, darlin'." He came a few feet farther into the space. "I told you to get rid of all this junk. Why are you keeping it?"

"Sentimental value. Besides, you never know when I'll need to furnish a new place."

His gaze narrowing, he picked up an old Tiffany-style lamp from the buffet, gave it a disdainful look, then returned it before gesturing to the open box at her feet. "You looking for something?"

"Just some old memories."

"What about more recent memories?"

"You mean from the night of the hurricane?" Did he think he was being subtle and she was too stupid to catch on? Or was she not worth the effort of subtlety?

She closed the flaps on the box marked Christmas I, settled back in the chair and folded her arms across her middle. "I know what happened that night. Why should I worry about remembering it?"

His strong fingers closed around the top rail of the other side chair, lifting it to a spot a half-dozen feet from her. He sat down, his legs stretched out, looking far too comfortable, and shrugged. "What did happen?"

"I waited too long to evacuate—because I could," she said in a jab at his attempts to control Jen even after they'd separated. "It was raining so hard that I had trouble seeing and driving. I assume I got confused and took a wrong turn, because I wound up at Timmons Bridge. The water washed my car off the road, but I managed to escape. Someone found me and took me to the hospital, where I woke up the next day."

"And you know all this how?"

She mimicked his careless shrug. "I remember the rain. My car was found near the bridge. I was found stumbling alongside the road a few miles from there. The rest of it is logical."

"But you don't actually remember any of it besides the rain."

"And waking up in the hospital with one hell of a headache," she added with a sarcastic smile.

"You don't remember where you made the wrong turn. You don't remember making any stops or how you got to the bridge."

She increased the sarcasm quotient. "If I'd known I'd made a wrong turn, don't you think I would have turned around and gone back? And where would I have stopped? At the video store for a movie? Maybe the liquor store for a bottle of wine?" She paused a moment, then softly asked, "What's with the questions, Taylor? Do you know something about that night that I don't?"

"Of course not," he answered, not too quickly, not too slowly. "I was working. I'm just trying to figure out where you went so wrong."

In marrying you. She shrugged again and took a stack of photos from the box to sort through as if the conversation held little interest for her. "I hit my head pretty hard when the car was swept off the road. The doctor told me I have traumatic amnesia and that my memory may come back or it may not. Since it was my first experience in a hurricane and my first car wreck and since I do remember how crappy I felt afterward, I don't care if I ever remember it all."

She made a point of looking at her watch. "Jeez, it's four o'clock. Quitting time. You probably have a date or something to get ready for. Don't let me keep you."

"A date?" He looked insulted. "Jennifer, how could you suggest—"

"I don't remember the night of the storm," she said sharply, "but I do remember the reasons I left you. Your controlling behaviors, your smugness, your arrogance, your women. I smelled perfume on you last night. What did you do? Leave her bed to come harass me?"

"Harass you? Checking up on my wife's welfare is now harassment?"

Interesting that that was the only thing he felt compelled to defend. No denial that he'd been with another woman that evening, no comment on the reasons Jen had left him.

"Estranged wife," she reminded him quietly. "What do you want?"

He raised one brow.

"Last night you said it's not over until you get what you want. What do you want?"

He rose from the chair and stared down at her, using his height to his advantage. She practically squirmed with the need to stand, to put them on a more equal level, but forced herself to remain still.

"I want what's mine." His voice was low, his tone mild, but he managed to convey a threat anyway. "If I don't get it back…" He returned the chair to its original place against the wall, then shrugged and finished. "You'll be very sorry, Jennifer."

As he walked out the door, the rain stopped and a beam of sunlight broke through the clouds, a bright shaft gleaming on his blond hair and tanned skin. He looked damn near radiant in the instant before more clouds dissipated and the sunlight spread.

Jessica watched him speak to Jimmy Ray, then climb into the Hummer and drive away. Though she was careful not to respond outwardly, inside she collapsed into a quivering puddle of relief that he was gone…and concern over his parting words. Did he consider Jen his? Or was it merely the evidence she'd taken?

And just how sorry was he willing to make her?

Though the rain had finally moved on, it was taking time for the water to run off through the town's overtaxed storm drains. Mitch drove slowly through a flooded portion of Breakers Avenue before turning into U Store It and finding Jennifer's car. He'd clocked out and gone home for a change of clothes before coming to relieve Jimmy Ray. He wished he could have stayed there. Wished he could go to his real home.

Wished he could take Jennifer with him. She'd be safe there—or saf*er*. She wouldn't be truly safe as long as Taylor and his bubbas were free.

He parked next to Jimmy Ray. The little bastard ground out his cigarette beneath his heel, stalked to the driver's door of his car, then scowled at him over the roof. "You're late."

Mitch muttered something physically impossible as he shut off the engine. Jimmy Ray flipped him off, slid behind the wheel, gunned the engine, then eased away, making the tight turn onto the east/west lane before peeling out with a squeal. Juvenile behavior for a juvenile personality. What was Taylor thinking giving him a badge and a gun?

That he'd found someone who shared his taste for crime, corruption and hypocrisy.

Jennifer was at the rear of the storage unit when Mitch approached, bent at the waist, tugging at a heavy box. Her shirt was pulled up, revealing a strip of pale golden skin above the waistband of her shorts, and the shorts stretched taut over the curve of her butt and ended high on her legs. Long legs with soft curves and nicely defined muscles, legs that had hiked for miles along the Great Wall, where she'd been impressed.

He was impressed now. Dry-mouthed. Thick-headed. Turned on.

She succeeded in heaving the box off the floor and onto a stack of other boxes, then she straightened and saw him. Wiping dusty hands on her shirt—not for the first time, judging by the stains there—she irritably said, "You could offer to help."

"Aw, gee, Miz Burton, let me get that for you," he drawled as he made his way through the mix of furniture and boxes. She stepped aside before he drew near, but he still caught a whiff of perfume in the musty air. He picked up the box and set it on a coffee table in front of a padded wooden chair. "What's got you in such a good mood?"

"The storm. The humidity. Creepy Jimmy Ray." She sat down and peeled the tape from the center seam of the box flaps. "A visit from Taylor."

"What did he want?"

"I asked him that. He didn't have much of an answer."

He looked around and saw another chair against the wall but left it there in favor of a footstool on big, fat padded feet. Its fabric was old, giant red roses on an ivory background aged now to the color of weak tea. Lou had had one very much like it in her bedroom, in front of the marble-topped piece she'd called her dressing table.

"What was it?" he asked as he maneuvered the stool closer, then sat down.

Jennifer folded back the flaps, took a stack of books from the box and set them on her lap before looking at him. "He said he wants what's his."

A muscle clenched in Mitch's jaw. "You?"

"I don't think so," she said drily.

"Something you've taken? Is that why you're here? To get it?"

Something flickered across her face—guilt?—before she began flipping through the first book in her stack. "I'm here because I've got to do something with all this—ship it, get rid of it, store it someplace else. I'm not looking for anything. Just taking stock."

He didn't believe her. If she'd taken something that implicated Taylor, that would explain why he hadn't been particularly grief-stricken in those weeks everyone had thought she was dead, why he'd made no effort to find her. It would explain, too, why he wanted to know her every move, as well as why he'd made no effort to reconcile with her. He didn't want *her;* he wanted what she'd taken.

So did Mitch.

Leaning forward, he rested his elbows on his knees. "Listen, Jennifer, you don't know what Taylor is capable of. Whatever you have, give it to me and get the hell out of Mississippi. I'll take care of it."

The look she gave him was filled with distrust. His suggestion probably sounded like a really bad joke to her. As far as she knew, he was no more honorable than Taylor—just one more dirty cop in a system full of them. She trusted him only marginally more than Taylor, liked him only marginally more.

And that stung. Stupid as it was, he wanted her to have faith in him. To believe in him. To trust him with her life.

For a long time they stared at each other. The emotions in her gaze were impossible to read, but he knew what wasn't there, and she confirmed it when she finally spoke. "I don't have anything to give you. I just wanted to look through my stuff."

Frustrated, he sat straighter. What could he say that would make her confide in him? Nothing but the truth, and he wasn't ready to share that with her. Not yet.

"You lived with him a long time. You know he likes things to go his way." He paused, watching for some emotion to cross her face. None did. She appeared absorbed in the books she was idly leafing through. "You know how he is when things *don't* go his way."

She finished with the last book, set the stack aside and reached inside the box for more. He grabbed hold of them before they cleared the top of the box, his fingers brushing hers. And there, finally, was some emotion. She stiffened, her eyes widened and she let go of the books, drawing both hands back, clasping them together in her lap.

"I can help you," he said flatly.

She unfolded her hands, knotted her fingers and crossed her arms over her middle. "You work for Taylor."

"I'm not like him."

"You work for him."

"Only because—" *Damn*. That stirred her interest. "He needed an officer. I needed a job. But legitimate police work is all I do."

"And spy on me."

That was pleasure, not work. Besides, he wasn't keeping an eye on her for Taylor. It was for her own safety. For his own peace of mind.

Uncomfortable with that thought, he forced a grin. "Hey, *you* invited *me* to the beach last night. And you didn't have to agree to have lunch with me today."

"I didn't invite you to come in here now."

"Do you want me to leave?" Not that he would go any farther than the car parked outside, but if she wanted space, he could give her that. At least a little.

Color edged into her cheeks. Ducking her head, she grabbed another armful of books, then focused on them. She'd paged through two before she finally answered in a very quiet voice. "No."

Her answer satisfied him more than it should have.

In the silence that followed, she sorted through another half-dozen books. Mitch watched her a while before speaking again. "Ship it where?"

She shrugged. "I haven't decided."

"Where are you going when you leave here?"

"What makes you think I'm leaving?"

"Are you staying?"

She traded one stack of books for another before shaking her head.

"Are you going back to California?"

The expression that crossed her face was sharp with sadness before she raised one dusty hand to wipe it away. "I don't know. With my sister gone, what's the point?"

"Doesn't she come back from time to time?"

"It's not the same," Jennifer murmured. Tight-lipped, she returned the last books to the box, folded the flaps to secure them, then looked around. Only about a third of the boxes were still taped shut; the rest were secured by folded flaps. Mitch couldn't shake the feeling that she was searching for something in particular, but what? And if she'd hidden it, why didn't she know where?

She gave the box a push toward him, and he obligingly got up and moved it to an empty space along the wall. After selecting a new carton, this one much lighter than the books, she sat down again, peeled off the tape, then combed her fingers through her hair. His attention caught on the blond strands, sleek, soft, styled away from her face.

She had wound up in the hospital after the accident, she'd said, unable to remember the events of the night, which suggested a blow to the head. That wasn't unusual when a car was swept off the road, though generally injury to the driver would have come from the front or the side. There was no sign of injury anywhere on Jennifer's face—no swelling, no healing scar, no fading bruise.

"Did you hit your head when your car went off the road at the bridge?"

She blinked once, as if the question had taken her by surprise, then grimaced. "Yeah. I had a knot the size of a grapefruit on the back of my head, along with one hell of a headache."

On the back of her head. Why? Her whole body would have gone forward or to the side until the seat belt or some object—the steering wheel or windshield—stopped the forward motion, and then she would have rebounded. The only thing the back of her head should have come in contact with was the heavily padded headrest. Nothing to cause a knot.

She could have gotten the injury after she got out of the car—slamming into debris carried along by the raging current or falling after finding her way out of the water.

Or she might never have been injured at all. Might not have even been in the car when it swept away. Might have made up the whole story.

Why?

He didn't find the answer while she rummaged through the remaining boxes. By the time she returned the last one to its spot, the rain clouds had gathered again, obscuring the setting sun, and it was getting hard to distinguish the rumble of his stomach from that of nearing thunder. But food wasn't his first priority when they finally left the storage unit.

"Leave your car," he said as she rolled the door into place and secured the lock. "I want to show you something."

Jennifer looked at her car, then his, and shrugged, skirting a puddle on the way to the Mustang.

The air inside the car was warm and muggy. He cranked his window down, started the engine and lowered the seat-vibrating volume of the radio. He didn't glance at her as they left U Store It, heading west to the edge of town, then turning north. She didn't ask any questions; he didn't offer any answers.

Their destination was on a narrow street that had once been the site of a small, private enclave of homes. The only way into the neighborhood had been gated, but that hadn't been enough to keep Hurricane Angela from destroying the homes. Nothing remained now but the street, in need of repair, and the bridge, seldom used.

He drove past rusted gates hanging crookedly

on either side of the entrance and followed the bumpy road to the incline leading up to the bridge. There he stopped and shut off the engine. The evening was prematurely dark and empty of the usual noises, as if all the critters knew another storm was moving their way and had taken cover.

Jennifer's BMW had been found fifty feet to their right, resting against an oak tree in a clearing that had once been someone's backyard. It had been muddy inside and out, dented and smelling of muck. The keys had been in the ignition, her purse had been on the seat and her luggage had been in the trunk.

But there had been no sign of her. And, apparently, no sign of whatever she'd taken that Taylor wanted returned.

She glanced around before looking at him. "Where are we?"

Did she really not recognize the place? Did she not remember turning onto this street, driving toward this bridge? Had she taken a wrong turn, confused by the storm, or had she come here deliberately, maybe to meet someone? To use the hurricane as a cover to run away with him?

He got out of the car, pocketing the keys, and waited for her to join him, waited so he could see her face when he answered. "This is your last known location in the storm. This is Timmons Bridge."

Jessica climbed the slope to the bridge, not stopping until she was in the middle of the span. It stood fifteen feet above the surrounding clearing, with woods on all sides and nothing besides the potholed street to suggest that there was a town just a thousand yards away. Weeds grew tall and lush, nearly obscuring slabs of concrete here and there, all that remained of long-ago residences.

The place was quiet, eerie. Lonely. But it *wasn't* Jen's last known location.

A whisper inside Jessica's head confirmed that. *I've never been here. I don't even know for sure where "here" is.*

"Then how did your car get here?" Jessica whispered back.

"What?"

The response came in an all-too-real voice directly behind her. Too late the fine hairs on her nape stood on end and warmth spread through her. Folding her arms over her middle, she casually moved aside, bringing Mitch into her peripheral vision. He was looking at her the same way.

"Were there houses here?" She tried to sound as if she were repeating her original question, but he didn't buy it. That was obvious as his gaze sharply turned on her.

He didn't press the issue. "Yeah. Until a hurricane washed them away. It wasn't supposed to be a big one, so they didn't evacuate. Eleven people died in the storm surge, including five children."

Shivering, Jessica lowered her gaze to the water below. Fed by rain, the creek was making swirls and eddies as it swept over logs that had lodged in the bed. A twig, its shiny leaves still attached, spun along on a dizzying ride, dipping beneath the surface before rising again.

Her stomach clenched, nausea rising. It was nothing, she told herself as she stepped away from the edge. Just hunger. The knowledge that so many people had died there. The combination of the storm just passed, the approaching storm crackling to the northwest and her own tension. Perhaps some sort of inner-ear balance thing caused by looking down on the rapid current from the bridge with no guardrails.

Lightning arced across the sky, followed by the low rumble of Mitch's voice. "How did you happen to come here that night?"

Her shrug probably looked as unconvincing as it felt. "I don't know. I must have taken a wrong turn."

"The logical route for evacuation would have been to head north on Ocean. To get here, you had to go south on Ocean, west on Main and north on Sandpiper. That's more than one wrong turn."

She heard what he didn't add: even an idiot would have had a tough time getting *that* lost, hurricane or no. Since she wasn't about to tell him the truth—that Jen *had* gone south on Ocean that night, that she'd gone to the house she'd shared with Taylor, that she'd never come here at all—she shrugged again and started for the car.

She'd gone barely five feet when Mitch caught her wrist. She stopped short, her entire body going stiff, and squeezed her eyes shut. She couldn't trust him. Jen had said so. Common sense said so. She shouldn't be out there alone with him, shouldn't be thinking how good that casual contact of fingers to wrist felt and damn sure shouldn't be wishing he would touch more of her than her wrist.

Slowly she turned to face him, difficult when every muscle was ratcheted so tightly. She wiped all emotion from her face but couldn't still the tiny quivers dancing through her.

"What did you take from Taylor? Where did you hide it? Why did you come here that night?"

"I told you, I don't have anything. I'm not hiding anything." Guilt pricked at her, but she ignored it. "I must have taken a wrong turn—or three or four."

"Damn it, Jennifer—"

Jaw clenched, she held his gaze, refusing to back

down one bit. She and Jen had agreed on a story, and she was going to stick to it no matter what.

No matter that she *wanted* to tell Mitch everything.

Wanted to tell him she wasn't his boss's wife.

Wanted to hear him call her by her name instead of her sister's.

His fingers closed around her wrist, no longer merely holding but touching. Flexing. Stroking. Tiny little caresses that sent enormous shocks up her arm and through her body. Oh, damn, she *wanted*.

The rain came quickly, not a sprinkle or a few fat drops here and there building to a steady fall but a torrent that soaked them in the space of a breath. Her cotton shirt clung to her. His dark hair flattened against his head, and his T-shirt molded his chest. Her breath caught in her chest as he moved a step nearer. Then another…or was she the one who moved?

His fingertips slid along her arm to her shoulder, her throat, her jaw, and he leaned closer, just a bit, his mouth almost touching hers.

Then thunder shook the very ground beneath their feet. Lightning brilliant enough to blind lit the sky, making the evening seem even darker in comparison. Making Mitch seem even darker.

A scowl tightened his face, and his mouth set in a thin flat line. With a mutter too low for her to hear, he lowered his hand, backed away, then circled wide around her as he stalked to the car. The breaking storm was a good thing for interrupting them, though she couldn't help wanting to be just a little bad.

Because getting involved with one of Taylor's officers was bad.

His car door slammed and she headed that way. Once she'd settled in next to him, he put the car in reverse and backed a hundred feet to the nearest abandoned driveway. They went back the way they'd come—Sandpiper to Breakers to U Store It—without exchanging a word. He stopped beside her car, and she climbed out, got into the rental and went home. His headlights in the rearview mirror were a comforting sight. The fierceness of his scowl as he let himself into his apartment wasn't.

Jessica shed her wet clothes, scrubbed her face and towel-dried her hair before dressing in the only outfit in Jen's closet that truly felt like the sister she'd known: pajama pants in pink and green stripes and a cotton camisole in matching colors. She curled up on the sofa, caught sight of the cell phone clipped to her purse strap and sighed. "I wish you were here, Jen."

Magically Jen's face lit up the cell phone screen. With a bittersweet smile, Jessica retrieved the phone and flipped it open. "How did you know I wanted to talk to you right now?"

"Twintuition."

Tears pricked Jessica's eyes. That was what their dad had called their connection—always knowing when one needed the other, one finishing the other's sentences, one sensing the other's feelings. Some people had thought it odd, but it was normal to them; they'd always had it. Always would, please, God.

"What did you do today?" Jen asked.

"I searched your storage unit. God, you have so much stuff."

"Hey, don't forget, I've seen *your* storage unit in L.A. Mine's not any bigger. It's just more organized."

Jessica grinned. Her office was immaculate, her records meticulous, and she never forgot a single detail of a business deal. But "order" wasn't her personal style. As long as she had a vague idea where something could be found, she was satisfied.

Then the grin faded. "What do you want me to do with all those things?"

Jen was silent a long time. "Keep what you want. Get rid of the rest."

Getting rid of the locker's contents had been one of the options Jessica had listed for Mitch's benefit, but the idea of actually doing so was hard to embrace.

"Don't be overly sentimental, Jess. I'm starting over, and you will be, too, once this is done. You know the important stuff. Toss the rest." After the smallest of pauses, Jen went on. "I take it you didn't find anything in all those boxes or you would have told me. What about the Don I mentioned? Any luck there?"

"Could it be Tiffani Dawn Rogers? She was a sixteen-year-old girl—"

"Who was murdered. It was big news. Plenty of photo opportunities for Taylor." Sarcasm dripped from Jen's normally sweet voice. "I don't know, Jess. I saw her around town, but I never met her. Why would her name be significant to me?"

"Maybe he had something to do with her death."

Jen was silent again, too long for Jessica's comfort. Her sister had seen Taylor's worst side. She knew what he was capable of.

"Maybe," she said at last. "I just can't remember." Her tone was distressed, and Jessica could clearly envision the expression that went along with it— brow wrinkled, eyes cloudy, jaw clenched.

"Don't worry about it," she said. "You'll remember or I'll find out. Either way, Taylor will pay." Then it was her turn to hesitate, to gather her courage, to find a believably casual tone. "What do you know about Mitch Lassiter?"

"He works for Taylor. They've been buds since grade school. Enough said." Then suspicion entered Jen's voice. "Why?"

"He lives next door. He's keeping an eye on me. I tend to see a lot of him." She shrugged and knew Jen could hear the action as well as another might see it. "I'm just curious."

"Oh, Jess, you *can't* be attracted to Mitch Lassiter. Take it from the queen of bad choices. You do *not* want to get involved with him."

"But you don't actually know him, do you?"

"Like I said, he works for Taylor and they're friends. That pretty much says it all. Remember what Mom used to say. 'You can tell a lot about a person by his friends.' You can't trust any of Taylor's friends."

But just the day before, when Jessica had accused Mitch of being friends with Taylor, his answer—*We have been*—had suggested that the friendship was in the past. That the only thing between them now was the job. And at the storage locker he'd said that he worked for Taylor *only because...*

She'd let that slide. Now she wondered how he would have finished the sentence. Because accepting Taylor's offer had allowed him to come back home? Because he couldn't get another job in law enforcement? Because he'd gotten into trouble in Atlanta?

"Jess." The impatience in Jen's voice made it clear it wasn't the first time she'd called Jessica's name. "You can't get involved with Mitch. You know he's watching you on Taylor's orders. You're too smart to fall for someone like him."

"You were too smart to fall for someone like Taylor," Jessica pointed out.

"Yeah, and look where it got me."

Sorrow welled, knotting in Jessica's throat. Look where it had gotten them both. She was masquerading as her sister, lying with every breath, trying to find evidence to punish a dangerous man and seriously close to falling for a potentially even more dangerous man, and Jen was—

"Promise me you'll stay away from Mitch," Jen demanded.

"Don't worry about me, Jen. You're right. I am too smart."

"Promise."

"I've already made you one promise, and that's

the only one you need to worry about." Jessica's fingers tightened around the phone. "Taylor will pay for what he's done, and so will anyone involved with him."

"Including Mitch."

The knot slid from Jessica's throat to her stomach, and a sour taste appeared in her mouth. "If he's guilty, he'll pay."

But, please, God, don't let him be guilty.

Chapter 8

Jessica awoke the next morning to the sounds of movement next door—water running, an occasional thud or bump. Mitch was over there in his sparsely furnished bedroom, getting ready for work. Showering, shaving, dressing. Was he in a better mood than last night? Did he regret touching her? Did he regret not touching her more? Kissing her? Holding her? Tempting her?

Scowling, she mimicked Jen. "'You can't get involved with him. You're too smart.'" Then she snorted. "Not smart enough by half." Because, even knowing what she did about him, she still wanted him. Knowing she couldn't trust him. Knowing he was looking out for Taylor's best interests, not hers.

She was an idiot.

As she got out of bed, Mitch's door slammed. Detouring on her way to the bathroom, she went to the window to peek through the curtains. The storm had moved on, the sun was shining and everything looked fresh and clean—except Mitch, who looked fresh, clean and cranky. The frown appeared to have taken up permanent residence on his face, drawing his brows together, lending his face a fierce air.

When he looked around the parking lot, she did, too. No sign of Jimmy Ray. He muttered something—no doubt a curse—unlocked his car, then leaned against it to wait. Then, finally he looked toward the window where she stood.

She was tempted to pull the curtains open and offer him a big smile and a wave. She didn't, though. She hid where she was, barely breathing, and watched for the minute or so it took Jimmy Ray to arrive. He was driving the unmarked car again, a brown sedan with two squatty antennas on the trunk, and he blew off whatever Mitch said to him—probably another obscenity—with a matching gesture.

As Mitch drove away, Jessica stepped away from the window. Now that she'd marked the storage unit off her list, the only place left to search was Taylor's house. A day like today, when he kept regular office hours, seemed her best bet. Who knew where he would be or what he would do the rest of the weekend?

But how to get there without Jimmy Ray following?

The question nagged at her while she dressed, did her makeup and cleaned the already-clean apartment. When eleven o'clock came and went without so much as a glimmer of an idea, she decided to go for a walk. Exercise always helped her solve problems.

The air was heavy with heat and humidity when she stepped out of the apartment, sapping the breath from her lungs. There was a stillness to it, a sense of anticipation—or was it foreboding? Was it due to the hurricane offshore or merely stirred up by her plans to break into Taylor's house?

Maybe it came from something closer at hand, she thought as Jimmy Ray started his engine and followed her at a crawl through the parking lot to Ocean. There she turned left, and he left his car, apparently realizing he couldn't effectively tail her that way.

Knowing he was twenty feet behind her, watching her every move, sent creepy shivers down her back, but she ignored them. No doubt Taylor had given him the same warning he'd given Mitch: *There would be consequences if I did anything more than watch you.*

She walked through downtown Belmar, first on one side of the street, then the other, gazing in storefronts, letting her mind wander. And that easily she found her solution.

It was in a tanning salon window display: a mock-up of a beach, with sand, an umbrella, flip-flops, a towel, a steamy book. She would never see a beach again without remembering the picnic she and Mitch had shared at Posey's Park. When she'd snuggled under the comforter the night before, she'd fancied she could smell both the ocean and him woven into its threads.

The beach was in the county, outside the police department's jurisdiction. Naturally, that wouldn't stop Jimmy Ray from following her if she drove out that way. Once she had him outside the city limits, it would take only one phone call to lose him for at least a few minutes.

A few minutes was all she needed to get lost herself.

She forced herself to stroll casually back the way she came. It was almost lunch, time for Mitch to replace Jimmy Ray for an hour, and escaping him seemed a more difficult proposition. She would wait until Jimmy Ray came back on the job.

She stopped at a hamburger stand half a block from the Sand Dollar, joining the high school kids in line to get a burger and fries. By the time her food was ready, Mitch had pulled into the parking lot and Jimmy Ray was trotting back to the apartment to get his car.

She waited for Mitch to get out and join her. He didn't. Too many people around, she supposed. He backed into a space, rolled the windows down, then shut off the engine. Dark glasses covered his eyes, but she could still feel his gaze. His hostility.

She understood the hostility. He believed marriage vows meant something and yet he'd almost kissed his boss's wife—and it wouldn't have ended with one kiss. She wished she could tell him the truth. Wished she could trust him.

But not until this was over. Even then, it might not matter, not if Jen's fears about him were proven true.

She found a small table shaded from the noon sun and lingered over her meal until the kids went back to school, until Jimmy Ray relieved Mitch. She felt the shift in the air when Mitch drove away, felt the sly, creepy aura that came off Jimmy Ray in waves. Time to escape for a while.

It took her less than five minutes to walk through the apartment parking lot and get her car. With her cell phone on the console, a number already programmed in, she drove out of town toward Posey's Park. When the trip odometer marked four miles, she reached for her cell phone, flipped it open and hit Send.

"Nine-one-one. What's your emergency?"

She injected every bit of drama she could muster into her voice. "There's a man following me! I've tried to get away, but I can't lose him and I'm afraid he's going to run me off the road! Please, I need help! I'm so afraid!"

She answered the operator's questions—a fake name, a description of her car and Jimmy Ray's, their location—and was rewarded within minutes with the sound of a siren. After thanking the operator, she disconnected.

When flashing lights appeared behind Jimmy Ray's car, she slowed, forcing him to slow, too, then watched in the rearview mirror as he realized that he was the trooper's target. His face screwed up and he threw both hands in the air in exasperation before moving onto the shoulder and stopping.

Seeing a turnoff ahead on the left, Jessica

swung the wheel in a tight U-turn and headed back to town. As she passed the two vehicles on the side of the road, the trooper was standing behind the brown sedan, gun drawn and barking out orders.

It wouldn't take long for Jimmy Ray to straighten out things with the trooper, but a few minutes' head start was all she needed—that, and a way off this road before he or his fellow officers spotted her.

She was headed toward town at ten miles over the speed limit when Jen called. "Your timing is impeccable," Jessica said in a rush. "I've got maybe five minutes to get over to Taylor's house. Do you know any shortcuts?"

"There's a convenience store on the edge of town that has a big orange and purple sign. Turn left there, go to the end of the street and turn right. How did you get away from your escort?"

"I called the highway patrol on him." Spotting the hideous sign, Jessica turned without touching the brakes. "Do I have to break into the house?" She hadn't come prepared for that, but she could make use of whatever was handy.

"No. There are some potted plants on the back deck, and one of them has a really ugly ceramic frog in it. It has a fake bottom and a key hidden inside. The code for the alarm is his birthday and mine—2817."

"Original." Her fingers taut, Jessica turned right twenty feet before the street dead-ended. "Where should I search?"

"Anywhere. Everywhere. I don't know."

"It's a good thing I like to snoop," Jessica said with a forced laugh. "I just passed a sign that said this road ends in half a mile. Which way do I go?"

Jen gave directions and Jessica followed them while taking frequent looks in her rearview mirror. Every time she saw another car, her muscles went tight, easing only slightly when she saw it wasn't a police car. By the time she reached the spot Jen directed her to—an isolated ramp that provided boat access to Timmons Creek—she was wound so tightly that she just might explode.

And she hadn't even gotten to the real part of this mission yet.

"Okay," Jen said, her voice breathy. "Use the trees for cover as long as you can, then get inside and—and search. Snoop. Find something, please, so you can get out of town."

"I'll do my best." Jessica clutched the phone tighter as she shut off the engine. "I miss you, Jen."

Jen swallowed audibly, then said, "Hey, I'm here. I'll always be here. You know that."

"I do," Jessica murmured before shutting the phone.

When she got out of the car, the air smelled damp and dank—from yesterday's rain, from the heavy undergrowth, from the nearby creek. She slid the keys into her pocket, then started across the clearing. Shells crunched underfoot and mud caked on her shoe soles until she reached the tree cover, where a carpet of soggy leaves and pine needles muted the sounds of her passage.

The trees lined the creek bank for several hundred yards before thinning out at the first house. Hands thrust in her pockets and shoulders hunched, Jessica walked with long strides along the edge of the water. Grateful for the lack of fences, when she reached Taylor's backyard, she angled toward the house. The bands around her chest squeezed harder as she took the steps to the deck two at a time. Was it breaking and entering even when she had a key? Probably, when she— rather, Jen—no longer lived there.

She didn't have to worry about legalities. If she got caught, Taylor would punish her. Period.

The ceramic frog was nestled among water-logged pansies and was, indeed, ugly, with bulging eyes and bumpy puke-green skin. Hands shaking, Jessica withdrew the key, replaced the frog and hurried to the nearby door. Half hoping Taylor had changed the locks, she fitted the key into the lock, turned it, then opened the door. Cool air rushed out to meet her, raising goose bumps on her arms and legs.

It took more courage than she'd expected to step inside, to close the door and type the code into the alarm keypad. For a moment she stood there listening to the sounds of the house and her thudding heart. With a deep breath, she moved farther into the house.

It was a beautiful place, Jen had told her, and she hadn't exaggerated. Intricate patterns in the tiled floor, commercial-grade appliances, extravagant wood trim. The furniture was top quality, the plasma TV oversize, the entertainment system complex. Original works by unfamiliar but talented artists hung on walls painted in rich hues, and plush carpets overlaid cool tile and gleaming wood.

A handsome, charming husband and a beautiful house. Jen must have had such hopes for the future she'd stumbled into. She'd suffered such disappointments.

Jessica walked through the house while formulating a plan of attack. There was no way she could search the entire place in the time before Taylor left work, so she would concentrate on the areas specific to Jen—the huge closet filled with expensive clothing, the bathroom done in shades of rose-hued marble, the small office she'd set up in a nook in the kitchen—and she began looking for something. Anything.

She finished with the bathroom relatively

quickly and found nothing. On to the closet. It was obscenely large and held more clothing than Jen could possibly have worn. Shoes filled the shelves on one wall; handbags occupied another wall's worth of shelving; and a built-in dresser in the center of the room was packed with lingerie, sweaters and plain silk tops.

Jessica looked inside and underneath every shoe that could conceal anything—a flash drive or maybe a key to a safe-deposit box. She moved on to the purses, systematically searching through first one, then the next, until she picked up a Prada bag that felt heavier than its slight size could account for. With excitement racing down her spine, she opened it and found out why: a compact, substantial in weight despite its delicate appearance. It was square, gold, with cloisonné dragonflies on the top and colored crystal beads providing a grip to open it. She'd bought the compact for herself in Japan, but Jen had loved it, so Jessica had given it to her.

"Oh, Jen," she whispered, tears filling her eyes. "I do miss you."

I'm here. I'll always be here.

But being there in spirit wasn't as good as being there in person.

After sliding the compact into her shorts pocket, Jessica returned to the task. Finished with the purses, she looked in every pocket in every garment, peeked down inside the dresses on their hangers and felt the pants from waistband to hem for a bump that didn't belong. When she'd finished carefully searching every drawer of lingerie and running her fingers carefully between the folds of the sweaters and silks, she straightened, frustrated, and took a long look around.

Shelves ran the length of the walls above the clothing and held hat boxes and other decorative storage boxes, all neatly lined up, their patterns and colors coordinated to the pale blue of the walls. Jen wasn't a hat person—but she'd never been a plain-white-bra person, either. A big floppy hat would go perfectly with most of the ruffly dresses in the closet.

Spying a stepladder tucked into one corner, Jessica pulled it out, unfolded it and had climbed the first step when Jen's voice sounded as clearly as if she were standing beside her.

Did I mention that, barring a major disaster, Taylor always leaves work at four? He says a seven-hour day is one of the perks of being the chief.

Jessica checked her watch. It was three forty-five. "All right," she said with a sigh. "I'm going now."

She returned the stepladder to its spot, shut off the lights and headed down the back stairs. The skies had clouded over again while she'd been inside, and the wind was whipping tiny white-caps on the creek's surface. Hoping she made it back to the car before the rain started, she reset the alarm, let herself out and locked the door. Instead of returning the key to the frog, though, she snapped it onto her key ring as she set off for the distant woods.

Thunder vibrated the air and lightning forked across the darkening sky, giving a sinister feel to the woods that had earlier seemed safe in their isolation. Swallowing hard, darting looks from left to right and over her shoulder, Jessica picked up her pace until she was close to a jog. When lightning glinted off her car ahead at the boat ramp, she heaved a sigh of relief and loosened her grip on the keys clenched in her hand.

She'd inserted the key in the lock and was turning it when something in the air changed. Goose bumps rose on her arms, and the hair on the back of her neck stood on end. Lightning about to strike nearby, she hoped but knew even as the thought formed that it was wrong. This was energy of a different sort—edgy. Angry. Far more dangerous than lightning could ever be.

Before she'd found the nerve to turn, a hand gripped her arm and swung her around. "What the hell are you doing?"

She didn't scream. Mitch had to give her credit for that, although she looked as if she wanted to. Her eyes were huge and wild in her pale face, and her muscles knotted hard beneath his fingers for an instant before going slack. Had she thought Taylor had caught her? Good. He hoped it scared the hell out of her, because if Taylor *had* caught her—

He swallowed hard before giving her a shake. "Are you crazy? Taylor's got every officer in the department out looking for you. Do you know what would have happened if one of them had found you here? Do you have any idea what they would have done?"

Her face paled a few shades more and her body trembled. He resisted the urge to gather her close, to assure her that she was safe with him. Truthfully, he wasn't sure she was. Since he'd spotted her car, he'd been so damned pissed that *he'd* trembled. She'd been married to Taylor for three years; didn't she have any idea what he was capable of?

"What were you doing at the house? What was so damn important that you had to sneak in there in the middle of a storm?"

"I—I—"

He gave her another shake, and her mouth snapped shut. Anger chased the fear from her eyes, surging through her, giving her strength when she shoved against him. "Let go of me."

He didn't. He felt better holding on to her

arms—felt relatively sure he wouldn't slide his hands up to her throat and strangle her.

"I don't have to answer to you," she snapped.

"Would you rather answer to Taylor?"

"I'm not afraid of him," she replied haughtily, but she lied. It flashed through her eyes—fear in its simplest form.

Mitch leaned close enough to smell all the scents that were her. Close enough to hear the soft rush of her breathing, to see the quaver of her lower lip. "You should be," he whispered.

That brought the fear back—not a flash this time, but settling into her blue eyes and the grim line of her mouth. When she spoke again, the anger was gone and her voice was quiet. "Let me go."

"What were you doing in Taylor's house?"

She hesitated, probably trying to come up with a lie, then flatly said, "Looking for something."

"The same thing you were looking for at the storage unit yesterday?"

"I wasn't looking for anything yesterday." She sounded weary of her own lie. "I was just taking stock."

"Damn it, Jennifer—" Releasing her, he held her against the car with one arm and patted her down, shoving his fingers into her pocket. Her face flamed red as she grabbed his wrist, but he managed to withdraw the object there despite her struggle.

He'd expected something important, maybe some type of computer data storage. Not a flat gold box with no room for anything inside but two mirrors.

"It's a compact," she said, snatching it back from him and curling her fingers tightly around it. "It was a gift from Jess."

He stared at her. "You set the highway patrol on Jimmy Ray and broke into Taylor's house to get a compact?"

"It used to be my house, too."

"But it's not anymore. You *broke* in. You committed a crime for a *compact?*"

"It was a gift from Jess," she repeated.

"I bet she'd buy you a new one."

"I wanted this one."

He dragged his fingers through his hair. "God,

you *are* crazy. A freakin' *compact*. You're lucky I was closest to the house and you're damn lucky I'm not—"

A staticky female voice from his two-way radio interrupted. "Mitch, what's your twenty?"

Without releasing her gaze, he reached for the mic clipped to his shirt's epaulet. "I just checked the residence again. There's still no sign of her there. No car, and the house is secure."

There was a moment's silence, then came Taylor's voice. "Where are you, Bubba? I don't see your car."

"I'm parked on Magnolia. It's hard to surprise somebody when you pull up in a patrol unit."

"Yeah, good thinking." Then Taylor's voice turned hard. "I want to know where she is, Mitch. I want her found. I'm home now. You can reach me there when you know something."

"Ten-four."

Jennifer was staring at him, confusion and something else on her face. Not surprise. Not trust. Relief? Gratitude? He didn't want her damn gratitude, but it was a start.

She opened her mouth a time or two, but before she found the words she wanted, lightning struck an oak on the far side of the landing, sending a limb crashing to the ground, leaving the acrid smell of smoke hanging in the air. The noise startled her and goaded him into action. Reaching around her, he pulled the keys from the lock, then opened the door.

"When you leave the parking lot here, turn right. It'll lead you around to the west end of Main. Take the side streets, go home and stay there. No stops for any reason, no more trips out today. Understand?"

Her forehead wrinkled in a frown. "I'm not stupid."

"At the moment, that's debatable." He gestured, and she grudgingly slid into the seat. Once she was settled, he closed the door, then stepped back to watch until she was gone.

His own car was parked down the road around the curve. He took a shortcut through the woods, got in and sat with his eyes closed.

Why the hell had Jennifer gone to the house?

He didn't believe for a second she'd taken such a risk for a damn makeup mirror. And she'd been missing for nearly three hours. It couldn't have taken her that long to locate the compact. What else had she been searching for?

The only ones who knew were Jennifer and Taylor—and, unfortunately for him, neither of them was confiding in him.

With a tired grunt, he started the engine, turned left out of the parking lot and drove down Taylor's street. His boss's garage door was open and the Hummer sat inside. If Jennifer had delayed ten minutes, she would have been screwed and Mitch would have been...

His jaw clamped shut, he drove on past and headed for the station downtown, parking in the lot out back just as the rain started. There he managed to avoid everyone and clock out before driving home to the Sand Dollar, where he parked a few spaces down from Jennifer's car.

Water streamed off the building and cascaded into the lot, overwhelming the drains and spilling over the grass to the ditch. Old Mrs. Foster, who lived on the other side of Jennifer, was standing in her open doorway, arthritic hands wrapped around a cane, a gleam in her eyes as she watched him wade through ankle-deep water to the sidewalk. "Nice day, isn't it?" she called with a broad grin.

"My favorite kind," he replied drily.

"There's another hurricane off the coast, you know. They say it's going to come ashore west of here, but they're wrong. My old bones say so."

Mitch had learned enough from Lou's old bones that he wouldn't be surprised if Mrs. Foster was right. Leonardo was currently stalled, but as soon as it began moving again, they would have the proof. And Jennifer would evacuate this time if he had to take her himself.

He nodded a polite goodbye to Mrs. Foster as he slid his key into the lock. Then he turned back. "Do you know if Jen—Mrs. Burton is home?"

"Her car's right there, isn't it?" Mrs. Foster replied tartly. "She came in a while ago. Just before the rain started."

With another nod, he let himself into the apartment, stripped out of his clothes on the mat in front of the door and picked up the phone. Taylor answered on the second ring.

"Jennifer's home," Mitch said without a hello. "And, according to the neighbor, she has been for a while." He didn't mention that Mrs. Foster's definition of *a while* was definitely different from his own and, presumably, Taylor's.

"Son of a bitch. Are you telling me Jimmy Ray never checked there after losing her?"

"You'd have to ask Jimmy Ray."

"Well, hell. You seen her?"

"Not since lunch." She had managed not to look out of place among all the high school kids at Burgers and Dogs, while he'd felt very much out of place—like some kind of pervert checking out the pretty young girls. Though there hadn't been a cheerleader or school queen there half as pretty as Jennifer.

"Hmm. So she eats lunch, goes home, gets bored, decides to go out and screw with Jimmy Ray, then goes straight home again? I don't think so."

Mitch gathered his dripping clothes in a bath

towel and carried them to the bathroom sink, then turned the shower on hot. "I checked your house as soon as Jimmy Ray called in and I stayed in the area. She wasn't there." Or so he'd thought. He'd parked in the driveway twice and walked around back, trying doors. He hadn't seen any sign of her. But after checking the house the second time, through sheer luck he'd found her car a half mile away. The fear it had raised in him...

"Okay, so she wasn't at the house. Where *was* she?"

Mitch absently rubbed the tightness in his chest. He had an ache in his gut to match and was getting one in his head. "She could have gone anywhere—shopping, to a movie, for a drive."

"Yeah, sure. But why lose Jimmy Ray first?"

"If you were a woman, would you want Jimmy Ray dogging your every step?"

Taylor chuckled. Mitch hadn't meant it as a joke.

"There'll be a nice bonus for you come next payday, Bubba," Taylor reminded him.

"Yeah, right," Mitch mumbled before hanging up. Who needed a bonus? He would watch

Jennifer for free, though he was pretty sure he would wind up paying for it, one way or another.

He was halfway through his shower when the power went off. He toweled dry in the dark, found clean clothes by touch in the gloomy closet and was getting a bottle of water from the refrigerator when a knock sounded.

At the connecting door.

He could ignore it. Jennifer was smart. She would get the message. But he automatically headed that way as if he didn't have a choice in the matter.

He would keep his distance, he promised himself as he twisted the lock.

He was probably lying, he admitted as he opened the door.

She stood in her own room, wearing shorts and a body-hugging shirt that buttoned from its rounded neckline down, and she held two bottles of cold water in one hand, a lighted candle in the other. Her smile when she saw he already had a bottle was only halfhearted. She set the second bottle on the night table, then put the candle there, as well.

She didn't waste any time on pleasantries. "Why did you lie to Taylor for me?"

He didn't bother making excuses. "He already thinks you're a threat. If he knew you'd been in his house, he would hurt you."

"The other people who work for him don't seem to have a problem with that."

"I'm not like them." He managed a slick smile. "I'm a cop. My job is to protect and serve."

"What if he finds out you lied?"

He would find out sooner or later. Mitch wanted him to know. "I'll deal with that when it happens."

"He would hurt you, too."

"He would try." But Mitch would be ready for him. He knew better than to turn his back on Taylor. He knew what his old friend was capable of. Knew what *he* was capable of.

Then, though he shouldn't ask, though it couldn't matter, he asked, "Would it bother you?"

"If you got hurt because of me? Of course it would." She raised her water bottle to her mouth.

Her hand was unsteady, and a few drops of cold liquid splashed onto the skin above the first button of her shirt. With a clumsy smile, she wiped them away but left a smear of dampness behind.

Without thought, he raised his own hand, rubbing his fingers over the moisture. Her skin was soft and warm. His was callused and hot. Together they damn near steamed. Her heart began beating faster beneath his fingertips, and heat flushed through her and into him. He should jerk his hand back, close the door in her face and lock it, then go for a five-mile run in the rain or, better yet, take a long walk off a short pier.

But he did none of that. He just touched her and enjoyed it. And if the hazy expression she wore was anything to judge by, so did she.

Though his hand was unsteady, the first button came undone easily—a little push here, a little pull there. A voice in his head—his conscience, sounding very much like Lou—warned him to stop. *She's a married woman.*

But for all practical purposes, the marriage was over.

The marriage isn't over until the divorce decrees it is.

She and Taylor weren't together and hadn't been for longer than Mitch had been around. She wasn't staying in Belmar and Taylor wasn't leaving. The marriage *was* over. And he wanted...wanted to touch her. To crawl inside her. To see her naked and damp and sweaty. To feel her every move, every breath, every quiver. Wanted more than he'd wanted in a very long time.

He slipped the second button free.

You always swore you wouldn't be like your father.

Gerald had refused to honor the commitments he'd made to his wife, to Mitch's mother and to the other woman in his life. Mitch hadn't made any commitments. He didn't have any vows to break. He was free to be with any woman he chose, and Jennifer was free to choose to be that woman.

The third button came loose with little more than a touch. Then she set the water aside and stopped him, her damp hand curving lightly around his, her fingers holding his still. "Can I ask you one question?" Her voice was husky, sexy, to match the look in her eyes.

"Okay."

"And you'll answer it honestly?"

His smile was thin. "I've been honest with you from the beginning." She was the evasive one, the one keeping secrets.

Her hand tightened around his for an instant, then she drew a breath and asked, "Would Lou be proud of the man you've become?"

He'd offered her one question at Down Home Q the day before, telling her he would swear on his grandmother's life to tell the truth. *Your grandmother's dead,* she'd pointed out, and he'd replied, *I would never dishonor her by lying.*

Can I trust you? Are you like Taylor? Are you one of the good guys? That was what she was really asking.

He was responsible. Trustworthy. Honorable. He'd learned all of Lou's lessons. He had values. Morals. He believed in right and wrong and consequences.

Even though he was about to commit adultery. *Separated ain't the same as divorced,* Willis had reminded him.

But Lou would have forgiven him this sin. She'd known about caring, wanting, needing until you hurt with it. She would have understood that Jennifer was different. Special.

"Yes," he said at last. "Lou would have been proud of me."

The tension that hummed around Jennifer vanished. She released his hand and moved forward, cupping her palms to his face, rising onto her toes, touching her mouth to his. Her lips were soft, her taste sweet, her kiss demanding. She slid her arms around his neck, pressed her body against his and thrust her tongue inside his mouth, probing, arousing.

Lightning crackled outside, and raw electrical energy of another sort crackled inside. It made the air hot and heavy—and it had nothing to do with the heat and humidity and the air conditioners that had stopped running with the power outage. It made his skin damp and sensitized his nerve endings so that the slightest sensation—skin touching skin, clothes rustling, hot breaths—became sharp, edgy, almost unbearable. Her hands moving down his spine felt like fire. Her breasts pressing against his chest was torture.

With the last bit of rational thought he possessed, he backed away from the door, taking her with him, pulling her to his bed. In her apartment, she was Taylor's wife—estranged wife. In his place, she was his. Plain and simple.

He slid his fingers into her hair and took control of the kiss, thrusting his tongue into her mouth, moving his hands over her back until he reached her hips. He lifted her, pressing his erection hard against her, his muscles clenching at the shocks that tore through him. He wanted their clothes gone, wanted to get naked with her, and suddenly part of that wanting came true. Her blouse fell to the bed, and a moment later a pale lacy bra followed.

He broke free of her mouth, lifted his head and drew in a ragged breath as he stared at her. Her skin was the same pale gold all over except for the rosy brown peaks of her nipples. Her breasts were round, not too large but all too tempting, and gazing down at her flat middle just made him want to get rid of the rest of her clothes. To see all of her.

The power of a look. Jessica shivered under the intensity of Mitch's gaze, a delicious sort of shiver that made her hot and damp in all the right places. He looked so fierce, as if he really wanted what he saw. Judging by the arousal swelling against her belly, he did want it—badly.

Holding his gaze, she hooked her fingers around the hem of his shirt and slowly pulled it up, keeping contact with his skin all the way up. When her nails scraped across his nipples, his breath caught. When she pulled the shirt over his head, he emerged with a lazy, hungry, predatory expression—and *she* was his prey.

She eased out of his embrace and walked the few feet to the bed. It was haphazardly made, with white cotton sheets beneath a tan spread, as if he'd slid out of bed that morning, given the covers a tug and considered the job done.

And now she was going to slide into that bed, give him a tug and get *this* job done.

At the bed, she stepped out of her sandals, unfastened her shorts and pushed them over her hips. When they puddled on the floor at her feet, she kicked them away. She was reaching for the band of her panties when his big hands covered hers from behind. He curled his fingers over hers, over the band, and guided her hands down, taking the lacy scrap with them. When they fell away, he released her hands and slid his palms over her hips, her abdomen, her rib cage, to her breasts, cupping them, teasing, tormenting. It had been so long since any man had touched her so intimately—so long that she'd been waiting for Mitch to touch her. Months. Years. All her life.

Thunder shook the earth, while his tongue tracing her ear made her shake. She reached blindly behind her, seeking the button and zipper on his shorts, getting distracted when her fingers brushed his erection instead. He was swollen, long, hard, and her gentlest caress made him quiver. When she worked her hand inside his shorts to touch him skin to skin, he sucked in a harsh breath and his entire body went rigid.

His zipper rasped, then he stripped off both shorts and boxers in one swift move. He tumbled her onto the bed and followed her down before she could catch her breath, his lean, solid body covering hers, his mouth taking hers in a greedy, hungry kiss. He left her only to reach into the nightstand, to fumble around until he found a condom. The instant it was in place, he sank inside her, filling her, stretching her, making her sigh with the welcome intrusion.

Bracing his weight on his arms, he moved inside her. There was nothing slow or sweet about his thrusts—just need, demand, lust—and she responded with the same, raising her hips to meet his, urging him with touches and whimpers to go faster, harder, deeper.

Climax came quickly, robbing her of breath, exploding through her body, tightening her muscles, then leaving her limp. Sweat slicked her skin, and her breath came in rasps while her nerves tingled and her body quivered. An instant later, the same reactions swept through Mitch as he strained fiercely against her, muscles rigid, eyes squeezed shut, panting, trembling.

He collapsed against her, forehead to damp forehead, and pressed a kiss to her lips. His body was a comforting weight for the moment he remained there, then he summoned the energy to shift to the mattress at her side. He lay on his stomach, face buried in the pillow. Though he didn't look at her, he touched her, his arm resting over her, his hand raised, his fingers curled possessively beneath her neck.

Jessica watched him peripherally—brown skin, dark hair, heaving breaths that were slowly returning to normal. The tautness eased from his muscles, but he didn't appear to relax. Tension of another kind—his conscience?—seeped through him. He thought marriage vows were sacred and yet, as far as he knew, he'd just committed adultery. How would that sit with the illegitimate boy who'd been called *bastard* one time too many? With the boy who'd seen first-hand the effects of breaking those vows?

More than anything, she wished she could tell him the truth, wished she could get him to look at her and say, *I'm not Jennifer Burton. I'm Jessica Randall and I'm not married.*

Could she?

Oh, God, she was tempted. She liked him—far more than liked him. She'd fallen for him quicker and harder than she'd thought possible. She'd believed him when he said his grandmother would be proud of him. She'd trusted him enough to make love to him.

But could she trust him with her life? With Jen's justice? Could she trust him to do the right thing? And, really, what did Lou's approval matter when Jessica had never met the woman in question? His grandmother very well could have taught him the shades-of-gray morals that Taylor liked in his officers.

Deep inside, though, Jessica didn't believe that. Didn't believe Mitch had anything more than a hometown and the uniform in common with Taylor. How could he? How could she have fallen for someone like that?

The same way I fell for Taylor, Jen whispered.

Suddenly Jessica felt very naked. She eased out from under Mitch's arm and sat up, swinging her feet to the floor, spotting her clothes scattered around at the side of the bed. She was about to stand when he touched her so very gently at the small of her back.

"Don't go," he murmured, then added so softly she barely heard it, "please."

He had repeatedly lied to protect her. He'd been worried about her that afternoon. He'd had plenty of chances to get her into trouble with Taylor, but he hadn't. He'd had plenty of chances to hurt her, but he hadn't.

And some part of her trusted some part of him. She wanted more, wanted to believe in him wholeheartedly, wanted to know that everything he said and everything he felt was true and honest. She wanted to know beyond a doubt that she'd fallen for the kind of man *her* grandmother would be proud of. But some part of her trusting some part of him was a start. For the moment it was enough.

She lay down again, turning on her side, facing him. Touching him. Wanting him. For the moment, having him. And she would make it enough.

Chapter 9

"I'm never going to live with Taylor."

Mitch was lying on his back, feeling as weak as he'd ever been after making love with Jennifer again, when she spoke. He glanced at her to find her in the same position, gazing at the ceiling. Feeling passionate about vows made before God was a good thing, she'd said. Did betraying those vows bother her?

Her hair was curling damply away from her face, and the flush of arousal was slowly fading from her cheeks and down her throat. She looked beautiful. Satisfied. And, yeah, bothered.

"Let's not discuss it, okay?" His tone was sharper than he'd intended, and the spasmodic clenching of her jaw showed that she didn't like it. He rolled onto his side and nuzzled her shoulder. "It's just easier to deal with by not dealing with it."

She gave him a ferocious look. "He has no place in my life."

"He's your husband."

"Not in any way that matters."

"In the *only* way that matters." Legally, her marriage to Taylor was binding. But that wasn't the only way that mattered. She didn't love Taylor. She didn't want to live with him, sleep with him, have kids with him. She didn't want to spend the rest of her life with him, and that counted for a whole lot.

What were the odds that someday she might want to spend the rest of her life with Mitch? Because he was thinking...

Too much.

Thunder reverberated the walls and the rain beat hard, drenching the already-saturated ground. If it didn't let up soon, flooding could become a problem in the lower-lying parts of town. Fortunately for them, the Sand Dollar was the high point in Belmar.

The air in the bedroom had grown sticky and hot. He rolled out of bed and padded to the window, pushing the curtains back a few inches, sliding the window open a few inches. The evening air was just as damp but cooler and smelled of rain. He leaned one shoulder against the wall and gazed out into darkness broken only by flashes of lightning. It was odd seeing no lights in the other apartments or in the houses across the park, no streetlamps, no bug-attracting lights shining down on the parking lot. For all the signs of life outside, he and Jennifer could be alone in the world.

No Taylor. No Jimmy Ray. No problems to solve. The idea held a lot of appeal.

Behind him, the springs creaked, clothing rustled, then Jennifer came to stand behind him, arms around his waist, hands clasped over his belly button. Her sigh was soft, melancholy.

He rested one hand over hers. "Having second thoughts?"

"Never." She rubbed her cheek against his shoulder, and he smelled perfume, shampoo, sweat, sex. "Storms just make me blue."

"I thought you liked them." He felt rather than saw her questioning look. "Taylor said once that you liked to go out to Sunset Beach and watch the storms from the picnic shelter."

Her muscles tensed at the mention of Taylor, then she shrugged it off. "Hurricane Jan cured me of that."

He didn't doubt that for a minute. She'd come out of the experience a changed woman. He'd never had the slightest interest in the old Jennifer, but the new one...

Not entirely comfortable that so simple a thought could stir the beginnings of yet another hard-on, he turned from the window to face her. She was little more than a shadow, her blond hair gleaming in some little bit of light, his white T-shirt doing the same where it stretched over her curves. "If Leonardo comes this way, you're evacuating."

Her look was steady. "To where?"

He didn't need to consider it. "My stepmother's in Georgia. Sara would be happy to have you."

She seemed to realize the importance of what he'd said before he did, based on the softening look in her eyes and the faint tilt of her mouth. He had never taken any woman besides his ex-wife to meet Sara and his brothers. The Calloways were family, and the women he'd dated had never been more than casual relationships.

"You can go with me," she said.

"Remember my job? To protect and serve?"

"You don't have to do that job in Belmar."

Nobody would be happier than him when that was true. "Right now I do." Before she could question him, he asked his own question. "What were you looking for at Taylor's house?"

She opened her mouth, no doubt preparing to offer the same tired denial, then suddenly went still. After a moment, her lips flattened in a taut line and she said, "I can't tell you."

It was better than a lie, but it stung anyway. "You trusted me enough to go to bed with me."

"Yes. But I can't trust you with this. Not yet."

"Jennifer—"

She gave his hand a squeeze, then pulled away, heading for the door. "My phone's ringing. It's probably my sister."

In the distance he heard the faint ring. She closed the door behind her, signaling her desire for privacy, and he respected it, turning once again to watch the storm.

He couldn't blame her for not trusting him completely. It had been his goal to convince everyone from Taylor on down that he was as corrupt as the chief—and he'd obviously succeeded. And when he couldn't trust her completely, he couldn't hold her doubts against her.

Lights cut through the driving rain as a vehicle rounded the corner and drove into the parking lot. Mitch didn't need the streak of lightning to recognize the Hummer and he didn't need anything more than the tightening in his gut to know it was Taylor. He cut the headlights, then backed up to the far curb and sat, presumably watching Jennifer's apartment. Did he not trust Mitch to do the job assigned to him? Was he planning a surprise visit? Had he found something out of place to indicate that she'd been in his house?

Mitch got the phone from the nightstand and punched in Taylor's cell. When his boss answered on the first ring, he asked, "What's up, boss?"

Taylor didn't sound surprised by the call. "Nothing much. What's going on here?"

"We're enjoying another storm without air-conditioning." Mitch paused. "It's a hell of a night to be out for nothing much."

"I have to go someplace anyway. Thought I'd just stop by and have a look."

"Nothing to see. I'd call you if there was."

Taylor didn't respond right away. When he did, it was with a chuckle. "Yeah. I'm sure you would. You seen her since you got home?"

Mitch closed his eyes. *Every luscious pale golden bit of her.* Guilt stirred inside him, but he ignored it. "No. She's been quiet over there. Except for her phone ringing a while ago, I haven't heard a thing."

"Probably that damn sister of hers. Jacki, Judy."

"Jessica."

"Yeah, whatever. Well, I've got to get going. Give me a call if anything comes up." Taylor disconnected and drove away. Just before the Hummer disappeared around the corner, the headlights came on.

Mitch returned the phone to its base, located his boxers and shorts, then pulled a T-shirt from the dresser over his head. Stopping at the connecting door, he listened a moment, hearing only a low murmur, before knocking.

"It's open."

His apartment smelled of dampness and sex. Hers smelled like something good enough to eat, thanks to the candles scattered around both rooms. She was standing near the dining table, cell phone in her hand, but it was closed, her call apparently ended. His shirt fell well past her hips but left a lot of long leg bared to his view. She looked incredibly sexy in it. She would look incredibly sexy in anything now that he'd seen her in nothing.

"How long does the power usually stay off?"

she asked as she laid the phone down and went into the kitchen.

"Could be an hour. Could be all night." A glance at his watch confirmed that it had already been two hours.

"You want a sandwich? I'd planned to cook tonight, but I guess that's out." Opening the refrigerator, she gathered everything she needed, then began assembling three sandwiches.

"Taylor was just here."

Her hands stilled for a moment in the act of spreading mayonnaise on the bread, then she went back to work as if his announcement meant nothing to her. "He's worried about where I disappeared to."

"Yeah. You sure you didn't leave any sign that you'd been in the house?"

"Relatively so. I just snooped into my s—" Abruptly she raised her fingertip to her mouth, licking off a smear of mayo. "Sorry. My own stuff. I didn't touch anything of his."

In Taylor's opinion, her own stuff *was* his. *She* was his. At least until he no longer wanted her.

Or until he'd recovered whatever she'd taken. If he let her live.

She finished with the sandwiches, placed two on a plate and offered it to Mitch. "Dinner is served," she said, then picked up her own plate and started past him into the living room. Halfway there, she turned back and gave him a sexually charged smile. "And if you eat it all like a good boy, there'll be something special for dessert."

He clamped his jaw tightly as she walked to the couch, sitting with considerable dignity considering that the only thing she wore was his shirt. She *would* survive this mess. It was enough that he had sex with a married woman on his conscience.

He wouldn't have her death there, as well.

The power came back on around three o'clock, the sound of the air-conditioning waking Jessica from sleep. The bedside clock whirred and flashed before resetting itself to the proper time, and the refrigerator motor hummed. Sighing gratefully as air from the vents cooled her body, she groped to find the covers…and found a body instead. A very male body.

Mitch. Raising onto one arm, she watched him sleep. She was in his bed in his apartment and had been for the better part of the night. It had been an incredible night, too. Long months of celibacy ended with a level of intimacy she hadn't shared with any man in too long to recall.

And he didn't even know her real name.

Jen had shrieked with dismay on the phone when Jessica had confessed that she'd slept with Mitch. *He's one of Taylor's bubbas!* she'd insisted. *He's playing you, Jess, he's lying to you! He'll turn you over to Taylor in a heartbeat!*

If Taylor had given her sister anything, it was skepticism in spades. The only person Jen trusted was Jessica. She didn't care that Jessica's gut said Mitch was one of the good guys. She didn't give any weight to the fact that Jessica was well on her way to falling in love with him. After all, hadn't Jen fallen in love with Taylor? *And look how that turned out.*

But Mitch wasn't Taylor. He *wasn't*.

Curtains fluttering in the breeze caught her attention, and she slid from the bed to close and lock the window. The rain had ended sometime while she'd slept, and the runoff that had filled the parking lot had drained away. Next door, her television was on again, along with the lights, and lights showed under Mitch's bathroom door. She picked up the T-shirt she'd discarded earlier, tugged it over her head, then went through the open door into her apartment. She did the bedtime routine—closed the window, took their dinner plates into the kitchen, shut off the television and the lights, then headed back to his place. She got distracted, though, at the last lamp, shining on the photos hanging on the bedroom wall.

She looked at herself and saw Jennifer. From the moment of their births, they had looked alike, talked alike, moved alike. They had traded places and fooled everyone, from teachers to boyfriends to parents—to a husband. They had developed different interests as adults and had followed different paths, but at heart they had remained the same.

This thing with Mitch—was it the same as

Jen's relationship with Taylor? Was it destined to end as badly? Or was Jen, to use another of their mother's expressions, once burned, twice shy?

She touched the lone photo of Jen, in shorts and a bikini top, taken on the cruise where she'd met Taylor, and tears welled in her eyes. "Damn it, Jen…"

Hey. No swearing. You know what Mom always said—it isn't ladylike.

Sniffing, Jessica turned toward the phone on the night table, its screen lit up with the incoming call. She picked it up and flipped it open, then sat down on the bed. "But sometimes it feels so damn good."

"You okay?"

"Yeah. I'm fine."

"No, 'fine' would be curled up next to Tall, Dark and Hot. Being awake and alone at three-fifteen in the morning sounds more like trouble."

"I just got up to turn off the lights. I'm going back to bed soon." Jessica drew her knees to her chest and rested her arm across them. "I really do think he's okay."

"For your sake, I hope so." Jen was trying to

sound optimistic, but she didn't pull it off. "Listen, when you were at the house, did you go into Taylor's study? Down the hall and across from the master bedroom?"

"No. I didn't have time. Besides, you told me you weren't allowed in there." Jessica grimaced as she said the last words.

"I know. But I keep seeing flashes of it—the furniture, the entertainment system. I know it's his study, Jess. I think I must have gone in there the night he—the night of the hurricane. It makes sense, doesn't it? Where's the likeliest place to find something incriminating than in his very own private room where no one else is allowed?"

"But for you to hide something there?" It didn't seem logical. The study *was* Taylor's private domain. He had constant access to it. Better to hide her find in one of *her* domains.

Though wasn't that the first place he would look?

"Maybe I didn't have time to get out with it. Maybe he caught me."

"Okay, so I'll look in his study. What does he usually do on the weekend?"

"If the weather's good, he takes his boat out or golfs at the country club. If the weather's bad, he'll get together with Billy Starrett and some others for a game of poker or—oh, wait. It's September. If the University of Mississippi has a home football game, he'll go. He played there, you know. He likes to relive the days."

Mitch had played there, too. Did he follow the team enough to know their home schedule? "Okay, I'll find out. If I can't make it this weekend, I'll try Monday."

"Thanks, Jess. I know it's weird, but I keep seeing that entertainment system. It's got to mean something."

"I'll check it out. I promise."

Jen's voice turned emotional. "Be careful. If anything happened to you…"

Jessica swallowed over the lump in her throat. "I'll be fine. Remember? I'm older, bolder and braver."

"And I'll always be younger." Jen laughed. "I love you, Jess."

"I love you, too." Jessica closed the phone,

and the screen went blank for an instant before the time flashed on. The signal strength, she noticed, was at its lowest. She couldn't make a call to save her life.

The words sent a shiver through her. First thing in the morning she would find out if there was a football game up in Oxford and then she would plan accordingly: get rid of Mitch, get to Taylor's house, search his study. She would leave a little essence of Jen on everything she touched, a thumb of her nose at Taylor even if he never knew it. But right now sleep was beckoning. In the bed next door. With Mitch.

She shut off the last lamp, switched off the lights in Mitch's bathroom, then slid into bed. He automatically reached for her, pulling her close, shifting to accommodate her body against his. For the first time in too long, she felt truly comfortable, truly secure, and she slept.

Mitch listened to the slow cadence of Jennifer's breathing for a long time before he spoke her name. She didn't move or give any indication that she'd heard. He said it again, louder, but still got no response. With a sigh, he rested his chin against the top of her head and stared into the darkness.

He'd heard only part of her conversation—enough to know that she was up to something. *If I can't make it this weekend, I'll try Monday. I'll check it out, I promise.*

And there at the end: *I'll be fine.* A natural response to someone saying *Be careful* or *Don't get caught.* Maybe *Don't get caught sneaking around Taylor's house again.*

Whatever she was promising to do, Mitch didn't intend to let her out of his sight, even if he had to handcuff her to him. Even if he had to go to Taylor's with her.

Even if he had to let Taylor get away with murder.

By God, he wouldn't let anything happen to her.

Mitch wouldn't have guessed that Jennifer was such a good actress. If he hadn't known that something was up, he never would have known by the way she behaved the next day. She made it through a lazy morning and a late breakfast before saying anything out of the ordinary, and even then it was so casual that it wouldn't stir anyone's suspicions unless they'd already been stirred.

They were sitting at the table in his apartment, the remains of his breakfast special—fried eggs, toast and bacon—on the plates between them, when she laced her fingers around her coffee cup and asked, "Do you ever go to the Ole Miss football games?"

Football. Not quite what he'd expected, but Taylor did have season tickets to the games and always made a big weekend of it. Not the sort of thing his wife would be welcome at. "Not since I graduated. Why? I thought you didn't like football. Or basketball. Or baseball, tennis, fishing…"

He would have missed the faint pink in her cheeks if he hadn't been looking for it. Was she uncomfortable with lying now that they'd been to bed? That would be good, though it would be even better if she was uncomfortable with subterfuge, period. "I don't. I just wondered if I was keeping you from a game."

"Nah. Taylor's the big fan, and I imagine he's already there. So much of his fun is in the partying beforehand."

There—a flash of excitement that she tried to hide by busying herself with the dishes. "He'll probably be out late."

"He won't be back until tomorrow unless something happens, like Leo heading this way— or someone breaking into his house." He waited until she picked up the stack of plates and utensils to add, "Which you're *not* going to do."

Her hands trembled, sending a fork clattering to the floor. He picked it up, set it on the top plate, then gripped her hands in his. "You're not going over there, Jennifer."

The pink flamed red. "I never said—"

"'If I can't do it this weekend, I'll take care of it Monday. I'll check it out.'"

Tension spread through her as her eyes widened. "You eavesdropped on my phone call?"

"I was lying in my own bed. You were ten feet away and you left the door open. That's not eavesdropping."

She pulled away from him, set the dishes in the kitchen sink, then faced him, arms folded over her chest. "You don't have to worry about Taylor catching me. He's out of town. He'll never know."

"What do you want in his house?"

Her mouth thinned, but she didn't answer.

"Who were you talking to? Your sister?" Considering that she'd ended the conversation with *I love you, too,* he wanted it to be Jessica. He didn't want to be jealous, didn't want to wonder if there was another man in her life besides him...and her husband.

She stared at him stonily.

"You were free, Jennifer. You'd gotten out. Taylor thought you were dead so he wasn't looking for you. You were with Jessica and you were safe. Why the hell did you come back? What did you leave here that was so damn important? Evidence against Taylor? Something to use in a divorce? Or something worse?"

Her lips were compressed so tightly that they were shades paler than their normal color, but still she said nothing.

Mitch was tempted to shake an answer out of her when a distant trill caught his attention. His cell phone, stuck in the closet. Not the one he carried every day, the one that Taylor and everyone else had the number to, but one that only a few people would call—people he would always want to talk to.

Giving her one last glare, he stalked around the corner and into the bedroom. To emphasize his point about eavesdropping, he slammed the door behind him, then grabbed the cell. "What?"

"Whoa, grumpy old man. Good morning to you, too."

Mitch dragged his fingers through his hair. "What happened to *I* call *you?*"

Rick yawned. "You haven't called in a couple days, and this is too good to wait. Did you know your girl has a sister?"

Mitch didn't challenge his reference. Jennifer was, for a time at least, his. Besides, he knew Rick didn't mean it that way. If he'd been discussing a man, he would have said, *your boy.* It was just the way he talked. "Yeah. Jessica. What about it?"

"You know Jennifer's birth date?"

"It hasn't come up," Mitch said drily.

"Actually, it is coming up. It's October seventeenth. You know Jessica's?"

"No, but I'm sure you do."

"It's October sixteenth."

Mitch could hear Rick's expectancy over the line. Rubbing at the headache settling behind his eyes, he said, "Okay, so they're a day and a couple years apart."

"Not even a day. Minutes. Jessica was born at eleven fifty-eight on the sixteenth, and Jennifer was born at twelve-oh-one on the seventeenth. They're twins, buddy. Identical."

Twins. How the hell had Jennifer neglected to tell him that? She'd talked as if she and Jessica were close—but twin-close...that was something he would have expected her to mention.

"There's something else, Mitch." An unusual grimness entered Rick's voice and knotted Mitch's stomach. It took a lot to make his brother grim. "Jennifer Burton is dead. She died the night of the hurricane."

His legs unsteady, Mitch leaned against the wall for support. It took a couple of tries to get his voice to work. "No way. That's not possible. She—she's in the next room. I just—" Had breakfast with her. Had an argument with her. Had great sex with her.

"It's no mistake. I have a copy of the death certificate and the obituary. She was buried a week after the hurricane, next to her parents out there in L.A. Sole surviving kin is her sister Jessica."

Her identical twin Jessica. Mitch's gaze jerked to the door that blocked her from view. It was Jessica he'd had breakfast and an argument and great sex with. Jennifer's sister. Not Taylor's wife. His relief was almost as great as his bewilderment. Why would Jessica Randall come to Belmar pretending to be her sister?

He'd asked the question a dozen times, but now he *really* wanted to know: what the hell was she up to?

His fingers tightening around the phone, he slid down the wall until he was seated on the floor. "What was the cause of death?"

"Drowning, with a secondary finding of blunt-force trauma to the head."

"Accidental?"

"No way to tell. She was alive when she went into the water—they found water in her lungs—but she could have slipped or something. Didn't you say her car got washed away in the flood?"

"Yeah. At least that was the story." No wonder Timmons Bridge hadn't looked familiar to Jen—to Jessica. She'd never been there before the other night. "Where was the injury?"

"The back of her head."

Right where she'd said. Not the expected place, he'd thought, for the type of accident she allegedly had.

"Why wasn't Taylor notified?"

"Don't know. The body was claimed by the sister and shipped to California. You'd have to ask her about it."

Damn straight he would ask her. "I caught her leaving Taylor's house yesterday."

Rick muttered an expletive. "Did she take anything?"

"Just a compact."

"A compact what?"

"You know, a makeup mirror. She said she wanted it because it was a gift from Jessica." A gift from *her* to her twin who was now dead. A lot of sentimental value there but not worth breaking into Taylor's house.

"You think that's what she was after?"

"No. She wants to go back today. She's looking for something, but she won't tell me what."

"Well, you can't let her do it. It's too dangerous. Besides, you've got hurricane problems again. Leo picked up a lot of steam overnight and is headed to shore about fifty miles east of you. Close enough for you to get some nasty weather."

Mitch glanced at the window, but with the drapes closed, it was impossible to tell anything about the conditions outside. "When are they predicting landfall?"

"At its current rate, early tomorrow."

"Okay." He shook off the numbness that had settled over him. "I've got to go. I'll be in touch."

"Don't let yourself get washed out to sea. It would really piss off Mom."

"I do my best not to piss off Sara," he said drily before ending the call.

For a moment he just sat there. Identical twins certainly explained his reaction to the prehurricane Jennifer versus the posthurricane one. He'd thought the storm had changed her—the trauma, the brush with death. He would never in a million years have guessed that she was literally a different person.

A different person so much like Jennifer that even Jennifer's husband hadn't seen the difference.

Finally he shoved himself to his feet, opened the door and walked into the living room. She was standing in front of the stereo, thumbing through the CDs stacked alongside it. She pretended great interest in a compilation of jazz greats while sneaking sidelong glances at him.

Still stunned, he studied her with the same degree of interest. He'd lived next door to Jennifer Burton for three months and he honestly couldn't see any differences. Maybe Jennifer's hair had been a shade blonder or Jessica's smile was a shade crooked—or maybe he was seeing things that weren't there.

He remained next to the door, silent and watching her, long enough to make her uncomfortable. She put the CDs down, slid her hands into the hip pockets of her shorts and turned to face him. "Go ahead."

"And do what?"

"You obviously want to say something. Go ahead."

There was so much he wanted to say that he didn't know where to start, so he just grabbed one of the many questions rattling around in his head. "Who were you on the phone with this morning?"

Her gaze shifted fractionally. "I told you—my sister."

"No, you didn't. I asked if it was Jessica and you didn't answer."

"Okay. I'm telling you now—it was my sister."

"Your sister Jessica?"

"The only one I have."

He folded his arms across his chest. "Tell me

one thing, will you? How do you have a phone conversation with yourself?"

For one long moment her expression was blank, then his question sank in. She shifted her weight from one foot to the other, swallowed hard and said, "Don't be silly. I was talking to—"

He raised his hand to cut her off. "I know about Jennifer. I know she's dead. I know you're Jessica. So tell me again—who were you on the phone with?"

Chapter 10

Oh, God.

Jessica's knees buckled beneath her. She moved the few feet to reach the sofa and sank onto its cushions. Part of her was relieved that he'd found out the truth, but part of her was terrified. If he could figure it out, could Taylor? Or would he save his boss the trouble and just tell him?

"Wh-what gave me away?" she asked, her voice little more than a breathy quiver.

"Nothing. My brother was looking into your—into Jennifer's background. He came across her obituary and the fact that she had a twin."

"Why was your brother—" Breaking off, she dismissed the question with a faint gesture. "What are you going to do?"

Mitch remained still, giving her a flat, intense stare, then spun around and disappeared into the bedroom. He returned with a small flat object clenched in one hand. Crossing the room with long strides, he sat down on the coffee table in front of her and extended his hand.

It was a black case, the leather worn from use. Her hands trembling, she opened it to find a badge affixed to one side and a photo ID on the other side.

Mitchell Lassiter was a special agent with the Mississippi Bureau of Investigation.

"Oh, my God," she whispered. "Oh, my God. I *told* her you were one of the good guys." The shaking increased until the case slipped from her grip. He caught it and laid it on the table beside him, then stared at her again.

"Are you investigating Taylor?" she asked, pressing her hands between her knees to hold them steady.

"Him and the whole damn department."

She could trust him. She wasn't being foolish, wasn't letting her heart override her good sense. He *wasn't* like Taylor. The relief was enough to make her giddy. If she hadn't been sitting, she would have collapsed.

"He killed her—Jennifer. Taylor killed her."

"And you know this…?"

Jessica drew a breath. Her answer was going to require a leap of faith from him. She hoped—trusted—that he would take it. If he didn't, well, she would just have to convince him. "She told me."

She'd thought he was still a moment ago. Now he was utterly motionless, even his breathing so shallow that she could barely see movement in his chest. When he finally spoke, it was with exaggerated patience, as if speaking to someone who wasn't quite sane. "She told you he killed her."

"I'm not crazy, but I do hear her voice. It's this connection, this—this twintuition. We've been together all our lives, even before we were born. We *know* each other. We communicate…I don't know…telepathically. Nonverbally. I don't know exactly how to describe it."

He considered that a moment. Then, giving no indication what he thought, he asked, "Who were you on the phone with?"

"Jen. Since she died, it feels more comfortable to use the phone. Less…freaky. For those few minutes, we're talking on the phone like we used to, like normal people. For those few minutes, I can almost forget that she's dead."

He wasn't buying it. She didn't blame him. She'd lived this odd life, and it sounded outlandish to her.

She dragged unsteady fingers through her hair. "When we were five years old, our parents took us to buy birthday presents for each other. Jen was with our dad, and I was with Mom at the other end of the mall when I *knew* she'd been hurt. I ran looking for her, and she *was* hurt. Some bigger kids had pushed past her on the escalator and knocked her down, scaring her and skinning her knees. When we were sixteen and my boyfriend broke up with me at a party, I didn't have to call. She knew I needed her and she came and got me. Those sorts of things have been happening all our lives."

She gazed into the distance, remembering that day more than three weeks ago, and hugged herself to combat the sudden chill. "I was in a meeting at our Hong Kong office when Hurricane Jan hit Mississippi. I'd been keeping an eye on the storm, but I knew Jen was smart. She couldn't master the waves when we learned to surf. She wouldn't try to ride out a hurricane. But suddenly there she was, inside my head, and I knew...." Her throat closed and tears welled. "I knew she was dead," she whispered. "It was as if a part of me was just gone. I ran out of the meeting and went straight to the airport, where I caught the next flight back to the U.S. By the time I arrived in L.A., my office had already gotten several calls from the sheriff's office in Lamar County. I got a ticket for the first flight to Dallas, then called the sheriff's office and he told me."

"Why you?" Mitch asked. "Why didn't he call Taylor?"

"When Jen got a Mississippi driver's license, she kept her old one, the one with her maiden name on it. It was in her pocket, sealed in a watertight bag along with one of my business cards that said 'ICE' on it." *In case of emergency.* Since graduating from college, she and Jen had been each other's primary emergency contact.

Now Jessica had no one.

"So you came to Mississippi."

The question brought her gaze back to Mitch. It was hard to say whether he believed her. Sooner or later he would have to. After all, her story was nothing less than the truth.

"Yes," she replied. "I identified Jen—Jen's body and I took her back to California for the burial. By then Jen had told me everything—that Taylor had killed her, that their marriage had become a nightmare, that he was involved in more criminal activities than any of the crooks he arrested, that she had hidden evidence that could destroy him. I came here to find it."

"What kind of evidence?"

"I don't know."

"If she told you everything—"

She gestured impatiently. "Almost everything. There are things she doesn't remember about that last night—where she went, where she ran into Taylor, what she did with the evidence, where he killed her. Dying caused a little traumatic amnesia."

If her last words seemed half as strange to him as they did to her, it didn't show. "So you searched the apartment and the storage unit, and that's what you were looking for at Taylor's house." He waited for her nod. "But you have no idea what you're looking for."

"No. But I'll know it when I find it." Even if its value wasn't apparent to her, surely seeing whatever she'd risked her life for would jog Jen's memory.

Silence dragged out, broken at last by a rustle as Mitch got to his feet. He walked to the window and drew back the drapes, and sunlight, sharp and bright enough to hurt, flooded the room.

"Taylor was working that night," he said, his back to her. "We all were, trying to move the people who had refused to evacuate to higher ground. I ran into Jennifer leaving the apartment and I told her to go to the community center. She said she would. When I got there an hour or so later, she wasn't there. Neither was Taylor. He and Billy Starrett came in about twenty minutes after me, both soaked, both..."

Was he picturing them in his mind, searching for anything to suggest that Taylor had just murdered his wife? Standing, Jessica took a few steps toward the window, then stopped, well out of sight of anyone outside. "Both what?"

He turned to face her. "Edgy. Hyped. I figured it was just the storm, having a real life-and-death situation, bossing everyone around. Taylor asked if anyone had seen Jennifer, and I told him I had. He seemed...hell, I don't know. I never thought his reactions to Jennifer being missing and possibly dead seemed right."

"Or his reaction to my showing up?"

Mitch scowled. "Yeah. What about that? If he killed Jennifer, what made you think he would buy you in her place?"

"She remembered running from him along the water. I'm guessing Timmons Creek. He tackled her—he used to play college ball, you know," she said drily, recalling Jen's comment about Taylor reliving his glory days. "She landed half in the water, and the back of her head hit something on the creek bottom. She struggled with him, clawed at him and even managed to hit him a few times. He hit her a few times, too, before holding her head underwater. She was panicky. She knew he was going to drown her. Then suddenly he lost his grip on her and the water pulled her away. And she drowned anyway."

"But he didn't know for sure. And the storm surge carried her body away."

Feeling small and empty and sad, Jessica nodded. Jen had died alone, killed by the man who'd sworn to love her forever. She'd been scared, terrified, but when she'd recounted the details to Jessica, her tone had been level, her manner matter-of-fact. She didn't feel pain or fear anymore, she'd assured Jessica.

But she did want justice. Not just for herself but for Taylor and everyone else he'd hurt.

Mitch's expression turned thoughtful. "When Taylor got to the shelter that night, he had scratches on the back of his hand. One of the doctors warned him about the germs that would be in the floodwater. He said he'd gotten them from some dog he'd tried to rescue."

I resent that.

Squeezing her eyes shut, Jessica rubbed her temples. *Not now, Jen, please.* This conversation was difficult enough without bringing her dead sister's voice into it.

"Okay. So Jennifer left the apartment and maybe went to Taylor's house," Mitch said, talking more to himself than to her. "She would still have access because he never believed she was really leaving him. She went inside and got whatever her evidence was, he caught her there, she ran and he went after her. He hasn't found whatever it was she took, and you haven't either, so there's a good chance it's either been destroyed or is lying at the bottom of the gulf now."

Jessica shook her head. "She hid it."

He looked annoyed. "She remembers that but can't remember where or what it is?"

She shrugged. Needing a change of conversation, she asked, "Why are you here?"

For a moment he looked as if he wasn't going to answer, but there wasn't any reason why he shouldn't, Jessica thought. He knew her secret. That alone would be enough leverage to make her keep his.

Finally he began talking. "There have been rumors of corruption in the Belmar Police Department for a long time, but no one has been willing to make an official complaint. I'm guessing they're too afraid of what would happen. When Tiffani Dawn Rogers died, her mother had no reason to stay in Belmar, so she moved to Georgia, where she had family. She believed cops were responsible for her daughter's death, including Taylor, and she repeated it to anyone who would listen. Most people wrote off her accusations as drunken delusions, except for one GBI agent—my brother

Rick. He contacted me and I opened a case. I figured the best way to find out what's going on within the department was from the inside, so I got my old buddy Taylor to give me a job."

"Then you didn't come here from Atlanta. And you didn't leave the Atlanta Police Department under questionable circumstances." The relief that had swept over Jessica when she'd seen his badge flared again. He really was one of the good guys. She really could trust him.

"I left the APD a year ago to take a job with the MBI. I've been living in Jackson since then." His gaze narrowed. "And the only thing I've done under questionable circumstances is go to bed with the woman next door when I thought she was married."

"But she wasn't," Jessica hastily pointed out.

"But I thought she was."

And he'd done it anyway. He'd wanted her that much. How special was that?

And what were the odds that he might still want her when this mess was over? That he might want her forever?

She'd known him only a few days, her rational side scoffed. But it wasn't the time that mattered, it was the feelings—and hers were pretty significant.

Her features slid into a frown. That sounded like something Jen might have said after breaking the news that she'd married a man she'd just met a few days before. But Jessica wasn't Jen, and Mitch wasn't Taylor, and while she wasn't going to rush into anything as serious as marriage, she would love to have the chance to see if that might develop.

"Remember I asked you about someone named Don?" She waited for his nod. "The name had been bothering Jen. That's why I was at the library, looking for something about anyone named Don. I found the news story about Tiffani Dawn, and now you say that her mother thinks Taylor had something to do with her death. That must be what Jen had found, something that links him to Tiffani Dawn."

"Maybe. He's involved in a lot of stuff. Embezzlement, extortion, blackmail, racketeering."

"And murder." Even if he hadn't choked the last breath out of her sister, he was as responsible for her death as if he had. And if he could kill his own wife that easily, how much challenge would a sixteen-year-old girl have been?

With a sudden surge of energy, she headed for the bedroom door. "We've got to get moving. It's already eleven o'clock. We need to—"

Mitch caught her arm and pulled her up short. "You're not going back to his house, Jess. It's too dangerous."

"He's out of town."

"He'll be back."

"We'll get in and out before he gets back. I have a key and I know the code to the alarm. We just have to be care—"

"Jessica." His tone was quiet, his hands gentle but firm.

Practically since they'd met, she had wanted to hear him call her by her own name, not Jen's—had wanted to hear how sexy it sounded in his deep voice. Sexy enough to send a quiver of longing through her. But not enough to stop the disappointment that followed, because it was clear that he wasn't going to help her.

"I want you to leave," he said. "Pack your stuff, load up the Mustang and drive north to Interstate 20, then east to Copper Lake, Georgia. Sara will be waiting for you when you get there."

Jessica went still inside. "You don't strike me as the sort to let others drive your car." *Or to share your family.*

"I never have."

He didn't say more, but he didn't need to. She wasn't the only one who thought this thing between them was special. Offering his car, his stepmother—that was pretty special, indeed.

And part of her wanted more than anything to accept. To pack the few important things in Jen's apartment and load them into the Mustang. To climb in next to Mitch and drive away from Belmar, the storm and Taylor. To drive to a place where Mitch was loved and she would be welcomed. Where they would be safe.

But he wasn't offering to go to Georgia with

her, and she couldn't leave anyway. She'd made a promise to Jen. And when would she have a better chance to search Taylor's study than when he was out of town? Even if he came back early, the storm would keep him occupied.

That's what I thought a few weeks ago, Jen whispered. *And look what happened. Do what Mitch wants. Leave.*

She couldn't.

But she could let Mitch think she was.

"Where is Copper Lake?"

Unmistakable relief flashed through his dark eyes. "I'll write down the directions while you pack. Go on. Get started." He pressed a kiss to her forehead, then turned her toward the connecting door with a gentle shove.

Ignoring the guilt that gnawed at her, Jessica went into Jen's room. It took only a few minutes to pack her own belongings plus a few of Jen's most casual outfits. Then she took the family pictures from the bedroom wall, wrapping each frame in a towel before stacking it in a laundry basket. When that was done, she slid her cell phone into her pocket, then went back to Mitch's apartment.

He was standing next to the kitchen counter, his back to her, the phone cradled between his ear and shoulder as he scrawled on a piece of paper. "I appreciate it a lot, Sara," he was saying. "I know you'll take care of her." After a pause while his stepmother spoke, he laughed. "Yeah, I'll worry about her anyway but less than I would otherwise. I'll give her your number and ask her to check in with you when she stops for gas."

That uncomfortable guilt flared again. It was wrong to lie to him, to pretend to accept his and Sara's generous offer only as a means to escape his scrutiny.

But Taylor had to pay. Jen's evidence had been worth killing for. The evidence Mitch was gathering against him would punish him for his other crimes, but Jessica didn't care about those. He had to pay for Jen's murder.

"It's about a seven-hour drive," Mitch was saying when she tuned back in, "and traffic's probably going to be pretty heavy. But she'll be there by tonight. Thanks, Sara."

After he hung up, Jessica forced herself to move. Hearing her, he turned, smiled faintly and offered the paper. "Sara's expecting you. Here are the directions."

She glanced at it—detailed instructions, Sara's address in Copper Lake and both his and Sara's telephone numbers—and wished she was really going to follow those directions. But she'd never been very good at doing what she was told.

She forced a smile that wasn't much better than his. "I'm looking forward to meeting her. I want to hear what kind of stories she has to tell about you."

"Sara loves me. She'll only tell you the good stuff."

She folded the paper until it was small enough to fit in her hip pocket. Movement outside caught her attention, and she gestured as one of the neighbors carried two suitcases out to her car. "Any chance you'll come with me?" she asked with forced casualness. Because if he said yes, she really would go. She would put off searching Taylor's house, would even consider settling for whatever justice he might face without Jen's evidence.

He shook his head. "My job is here."

"You're not really a Belmar cop."

"No, but I'm being paid to act like one." Sliding his arm around her shoulders, he walked with her back to Jen's room. "Call Sara when you stop."

"I will."

"Call me before you call Sara."

She swallowed hard. "I will."

"Don't forget your slicker. You'll probably get caught in the rain." He picked up her suitcase, then braced the basket against his hip and carried both outside to the car. After detouring to get the blue slicker from the closet, Jessica followed.

The sun was shining and the humidity was thick, like a normal September day in southern Mississippi, but there was tension in the air. No breeze blew, no kids played in the park, no one was out enjoying the weekend. Even if she didn't know Hurricane Leo was off the coast, she would still know something was wrong.

Mitch put the luggage in the trunk, then offered her the keys. She hesitated, and when she did reach out, he closed his fingers around hers and pulled her close. Her fingers were cool in spite of the heat. His were warm.

"Someone might see us," she remarked.

"Someone might." His other arm snaked around her waist, pulling her snugly against him.

"They might tell Taylor."

"They might. But you're not his wife, so it's none of his business. Besides—" he kissed her forehead, her cheek, her jaw "—Taylor's going to prison."

She hoped so and she hoped every day was utter misery until they finally put a needle in his arm. It would be a more peaceful death than he deserved, but at least he would be dead. Jen's death would have been avenged.

Mitch gave her a real kiss, the kind that curled everything inside her and raised her temperature to steaming, that made her want to cling to him for the support her weak knees couldn't give. He ended it before she was ready, put her away from him before she was steady. "You'd better go."

She opened the door and tossed her purse onto the passenger seat. "You can still change your mind and go with me."

He shook his head. She'd known he would.

"Be careful."

He grinned. "I always am."

With her stomach knotted and her palms damp, she slid behind the wheel and closed the door. The engine rumbled to life on the first try. She backed out, gave him a smile and a tiny wave, then drove off. She turned north out of the parking lot as if she were following his orders, drove past the grocery store and the building supply store with their parking lots packed. Apparently a lot of people were sticking around to see what Leo could do.

And she was one of them, she grimly acknowledged as she turned left at the next corner and started a circuitous route to the boat landing on Timmons Creek.

As soon as Jessica had driven away, Mitch had changed into jeans and a black T-shirt that said

Police across the back, holstered his pistol on his belt and clipped his badge there, as well, then made the short walk downtown to pick up his patrol unit. Billy Starrett, in charge until Taylor got back, had sent him to knock and talk—knock at the door, explain the situation and help the residents leave, if necessary—in Belmar's most affluent neighborhood, Taylor's. Save the rich folks first and let the poor fend for themselves. That was Taylor's motto, he thought with disgust as he climbed the steps of a beachfront Creole cottage.

The sun had disappeared behind dark, threatening clouds a while earlier. Now the rain started. He rang the bell a couple of times, then tried the heavy brass knocker. There was no answer. These lucky citizens were already gone.

It was the last house on the block. His car was parked across the street—he'd gone up that side first, then doubled back—so he jogged down the sidewalk and to the car. Every house he'd gone to so far, like this one, had been empty. He was wasting his time when he could be doing something that really mattered, like giving rides to the shelter to people who actually needed help. Forget Billy's orders. One more block full of expensive homes, and then he was heading to the north side of town.

Taylor's neighbors across the street were in the process of leaving when he approached. Mitch carried three heavy suitcases to the Cadillac SUV in the driveway, watched them back out, then started toward the next house— when something stopped him in his tracks.

He took a slow look around. Nothing was obviously out of place. The driveways were empty, and anything susceptible to high winds— planters, chairs, tables—had been moved inside. The afternoon had turned dark enough for the streetlights to come on, and lights burned in every house on the block. Any burglars who were willing to brave the storm wouldn't be deterred by a few lights inside, but it seemed to make the home owners feel more secure.

His gaze stopped on Taylor's house. Like the others, lights shone in several windows, including one upstairs. As he studied it, a shadow moved across the curtains from left to right, then back again, slender, of average height. Too slender, too short for Taylor.

His gut clenching, Mitch fumbled for the mic inside his slicker. He called the dispatcher, asked if Taylor was back in town yet and received a negative reply.

It must have been Jessica.

He crossed the street with long strides, climbed the steps to the porch and turned the knob. It didn't open. Back out into the rain for a quick jog around the house to the back. The kitchen lights cast pale angles across the deck, and a glance through the windows showed an electric-blue slicker hanging on the doorknob and a green light on the alarm panel indicating that the system was disarmed.

He swore long and loud as he slowly turned the knob. The door swung open without a sound. He shucked his own slicker just inside, leaving it to puddle on the floor. Hers was dry, which meant she'd broken in before the rain had started.

Of course she had, he thought grimly. She had

come straight there from the apartment. He'd been relieved to know that she was safely on her way to Sara's, putting more distance between her and Taylor with every minute—and the whole time she'd been here in Taylor's house. She'd played Mitch for a fool.

His running shoes squeaked on the tile as he crossed to the hallway. Dim lights burned in the living room and the foyer, where a glance out the window showed that the street was still quiet. Dimmer light filtered down the stairs, enough to illuminate his path. With gun drawn, he stealthily climbed the stairs, sticking close to the wall, keeping his gaze on the landing above.

Four doors opened off the landing, and the light came from the closest one. It was partially closed, but he could see enough to realize that it was an office. Taylor's private office.

He eased to the door, seeing more of the desk, file cabinets and a computer with a picture of Taylor's boat as a screen saver. Even from a distance, he could see the name painted above the waterline: Lucky. Fitting. Taylor had been lucky to get away with all his crimes. But everyone's luck ran out after a while. His was about to.

So was Jessica's.

With his free hand, Mitch pushed the door inward. It moved easily for a few inches, then suddenly slammed back into his arm, cracking against his elbow. Gritting his teeth against the pain, he stepped into the room, gun raised, and kicked the door shut.

Jessica stood two feet in front of him, face pale, eyes wide. Her gaze darted around—looking for an escape route? a weapon?—in the instant before she recognized him. Hand raised to her chest, she gave a laugh that could have as easily been a sob. "Oh, my God, you scared me!"

She was supposed to be a couple hours north of there, well on her way to safety, and instead she'd sneaked back to Taylor's house, broken in and was searching his office. And *he'd* scared *her?*

He holstered the pistol before she could notice that his hand was shaking, then fixed a glare on her. "You lied to me."

Her shrug was jerky. "I've been lying to you since the day we met. But it's for a good cause."

"Getting yourself killed?"

"I'm not going to die."

"It's a distinct possibility. If Taylor catches you…" He didn't want to finish the sentence. Didn't want to even think about what would happen if Taylor found her there. If Rhonda Rogers was right about her daughter's death, if Jessica was right about Jennifer's death, Taylor was a cold-blooded killer. If he could kill his wife, he would have no problem with killing her sister.

And his old friend. Because there was no way Jessica was going to become another of Taylor's victims as long as Mitch lived.

"We've got to get out of here." He reached for her arm, but she shrank back. He swore under his breath. "I'm building a case against Taylor, Billy, Jimmy Ray and a dozen others. They're going to be indicted. They're going to spend a hell of a lot of time in prison. That's enough, Jessy."

"It's not," she argued. "He killed my sister,

Mitch! She was all I had and he took her life. He's got to pay for that."

"We can't make him pay for it. No one knows what happened. There are no witnesses. No weapon. No evidence. We can't even show that Jennifer was murdered. Her autopsy was inconclusive. There's no way to prove that the blow to the head and the drowning weren't accidental. But he'll go to prison for the crimes we *can* prove. You'll have to be satisfied with that."

She began shaking her head before he finished. "Even if we can't prove that he killed Jen, if the evidence she had helps send him to prison, *then* I'll be satisfied. And it's here in this room. It has to be."

He glanced around the room. It was about twelve by sixteen feet, with bookcases and an entertainment system on adjacent walls. The floor was hardwood covered by a Persian rug, and the desk and file cabinets were massive oak pieces. The leather chairs were overstuffed for comfort, and the bar that occupied one corner was, no doubt, another source of comfort.

He could haul Jessica out of the house—most

likely, judging by her look, over his shoulder. He could get her back to the car, maybe even back to the apartment, but he couldn't make her stay there. He couldn't make her stay away from here.

Or he could help her search. If she found Jennifer's mystery evidence, great. If they were thorough and didn't find it, she would have to accept that there was nothing to find. She would have to be satisfied knowing that Taylor was locked away, even if it wasn't for the most important of his crimes.

"Where have you looked?" he asked and saw surprise flash through her eyes.

With a surge of nervous energy, she moved away from the bar she'd been examining and went to stand in the middle of the room. "I've been through his desk and the entertainment center. I've checked every book on the shelves and skimmed through the files in the cabinets. I've even looked under the rug and beneath the chair cushions."

"What about the closet?" The door was on the wall opposite the desk, stained dark to match the rest of the trim, its knob shiny brass.

"It's locked. I was saving it for last."

He crossed to the desk, opened the center drawer and fished out a large paper clip, then straightened it as he circled to the closet door. "What exactly are you looking for?"

"I don't know. Papers. Records. A flash drive. CDs." She shrugged helplessly. "Jen doesn't remember."

That made him look at her. "You're still talking to her?"

She nodded.

He hadn't given much thought to her claim that she was communicating with her dead sister—hadn't wanted to think too much about it. It was too weird. Dead was dead. Lou had never visited him after her death. Gerald hadn't been in touch with Sara or their sons. Of course, Lou probably figured she'd told him everything he needed to know while she was alive. And if Gerald could reach out to someone from the grave, it probably wouldn't be the family he'd betrayed.

But talking to your dead sister—by cell phone,

no less...he was too skeptical to accept it whole-heartedly and too smart to rule it out as impossible, but it was too damn weird for his own comfort.

The knob lock on the closet door was a standard assembly. Mitch inserted the straightened wire of the paper clip into the hole and popped open the lock, then opened the door. The space was clean, neat and empty for the most part. A couple of raid jackets hung on one clothes rod at the back, Taylor's football jerseys from his college freshman year hung on the other rod and a file box on the floor held a bunch of papers, wrinkled and faded from a dunk in water. One shelf held a digital camera, a digital camcorder and a tripod, and on the other shelf was a row of DVDs in clear jewel cases.

"Amber, Stephanie, Maria, Lisa, Laurel, Megan," he read aloud. Not that he needed confirmation that the dispatcher was having an affair with Taylor, but there it was.

Drawn by his voice, Jessica came to the door. "Who are you talking about?"

He gestured to the DVDs, and her nose

wrinkled in delicate distaste. "He tapes his sexual encounters?"

"Apparently." He selected one with an unfamiliar name and took it to the entertainment center. It took a couple of tries to get the proper components turned on, then he pressed Play.

His jaw tightened. He might not have known the woman, but the location of the video was all too familiar: an interrogation room at the Belmar police station. The cameras were there to tape interviews and confessions, not sexual liaisons. And it wasn't just Taylor's liaison. Billy Starrett was taking his turn with the apparently willing woman, as well.

Grimly he stopped and ejected the DVD, returning it to its case. Beside him, Jessica's cheeks were pink, but he thought it was more from anger than embarrassment. After all, it was her sister Taylor had betrayed.

"Did Jennifer know about this?" he asked as he put the DVD back on the shelf.

"She knew he was unfaithful. She didn't know he—" The color drained from Jessica's face.

"There aren't any DVDs in there with Jen's name, are there?"

He ran through the list again, then shook his head. Maybe sex with his wife had lacked the clandestine factor that made it worth preserving for future viewing.

Still pale, Jessica hugged her arms to her chest. She looked lost, sad, but not for long. Slowly her attention focused, her gaze locking on the entertainment center. "Jen said she keeps seeing flashes of this room, of that in particular. She was sure it meant something."

He looked at the cabinet. It was oak, to match the other wood, and its molding reached nearly to the ceiling. The shelves held a flat-panel television, a DVD/VCR player, stereo components and a high-tech sound system. A glance behind the cabinet doors revealed blank discs and tapes as well as prerecorded ones, along with a vast selection of CDs. "Maybe she hated keeping all this dusted."

Jessica snorted. "Taylor cleaned it himself. She wasn't allowed to step inside."

"Didn't she think that was odd?" Mitch couldn't imagine a man declaring any part of his house off-limits to his wife—or the wife who would let him. Jessica certainly wouldn't.

"Of course she did. But she loved him and she thought everyone needed a space that was their own."

Her scowl was fierce enough to make him steer back to the subject. "You said you searched this."

"Every bit. But maybe I missed something. Jen's just so sure…."

He looked from her back to the entertainment center, then began a methodical search, looking under, behind and inside everything. Jessica did the same at the other end.

The wind was picking up when they met in the middle, and the sky was darker. Mitch wondered idly whether Leo had picked up speed or shifted course. Either way, it was about time for them to get out.

"Is there anyplace left to look?"

Jessica turned in a slow circle. When she faced him again, her expression was dejected. She'd been so sure she would find something, and now that it hadn't happened, she looked as if she didn't know what to do next. "No," she said at last. "We've looked everywhere."

"We'll still get Taylor."

"But not for murder."

"No," he admitted. "Probably not." He waited a minute before offering his hand. "We need to go."

She ignored his hand and moved closer to wrap her arms around him. He rested his chin on the top of her head and held her close, stroking her back, easing the tension that knotted her shoulders. He liked the way she leaned against him, liked the way she felt against him. He could imagine not having her, but he preferred not to, at least for the next fifty or sixty years.

After a time she lifted her head and stepped back, and he let her go. "Okay," she murmured. "I'm ready."

He watched her walk toward the door, then turned to shut off the desk lamp. When he turned back, his gaze swept across the entertainment center one last time. It had been custom-built, like everything else in the house, as Taylor had mentioned on more than one occasion, but it didn't fill its space. The crown molding should have gone all the way to the ceiling, as it did on the bookcases. With that few inches' gap, the entertainment center looked short, not quite right.

Gaze narrowed, he compared its height to Jessica's. The cabinet was tall but not so tall that she couldn't reach the opening above the molding if she stretched. "Did you look on top?"

Jessica faced him from the doorway. "On top of what?"

He crossed to the wall in two strides, reached up and over the crown and down to the surface of the cabinet. His first few gropes found only dust, then his fingers brushed something solid. Thin. Plastic. He pulled it out, wiped the dust on his jeans, then held it up for Jessica to see.

It was a DVD in a clear case and it was labeled with Tiffani Dawn Rogers's name and a date.

One day after she'd disappeared.

* * *

Jessica's stomach roiled and her feet became rooted to the floor. *That* was what Jen had discovered, what Taylor wanted back so desperately: proof that connected him to the sixteen-year-old girl. And her murder?

Silently Mitch turned on the television and put the disc in the DVD player. The audio was muted, and from her vantage point, all she could see was a blur of movement on the TV screen. But one look at Mitch's face told her it was bad. Woodenly she forced one foot ahead of the other, half stumbling across the room until she stood beside him.

The location was the same room as the other video, with off-white walls, a wooden table and a large interior window with blinds. Black letters on the frosted glass in the door were backward but still clearly visible through the glass: Interrogation 1. It was in the police station.

Tiffani Dawn lay on her back on the table, naked, her eyes glazed, her struggles sluggish. Her arms were stretched out to her sides, each wrist cuffed to a table leg. Clearly she was drunk or drugged, but that didn't matter to Jimmy Ray, who was on top of her, inside her. Or to the men who watched: Billy Starrett and Taylor.

Jessica wanted to cry, to throw up, to kill the three men herself. They were police officers, sworn to protect, and they'd raped a sixteen-year-old girl. Had they killed her to keep her quiet or had that been part of their sick game, as well?

Unable to watch the screen any longer, she shifted her gaze to Mitch. His brows were drawn together, his jaw was clenched and his eyes were darker than night. Anger and loathing radiated off him in waves, along with something else: impotence. Tiffani Dawn was dead. He couldn't help her now. No one could.

Jess!

The voice was so real that Jessica automatically glanced around before realizing it was in her head.

Taylor's back! You've got to get out of here. If he finds you, he'll kill you!

Jessica raced to the window in time to watch Taylor's Hummer turn into the driveway. In the dim light she could make out two people inside—Taylor and probably Billy Starrett. Spinning around, she grabbed Mitch's arm. "We've got to go!"

She tried to pull him toward the door, but he headed for the DVD player instead. He removed the disc and popped it back into its case, slid it over the crown molding once more, then shut off the TV.

As they reached the hallway, the front door slammed. "I'm gonna get a beer," Billy said. "You want one?"

"Yeah, get it, will you?" Taylor's voice came from the stairs, punctuated by footfalls.

Jessica's heart kicked into triple time. They couldn't use the front stairs, and the odds of making it to the back stairs without being seen were nil. Even if they did, the stairs led directly to the kitchen, directly to Billy.

Mitch drew her silently back into the study, pushing her into the narrow space beneath the corner bar. She couldn't see where he went, but an instant later she heard the soft click of the closet door closing. Only an instant after that,

Taylor came into the room. He stopped abruptly and murmured, "Son of a bitch."

Had they left anything out of place? Jessica tried frantically to remember. She'd been careful to put everything back where she'd found it. The lamp was off, the television was off and the DVD player... Mitch had removed the disc and put it in its case, but she couldn't remember if he'd closed the tray.

A leathery creak broke the silence. Was that the sound a holster made when the weapon it held was drawn? Jessica's heart was thudding, and her lungs were too constricted to draw more than the smallest breaths. Taylor knew something was wrong. It was just a matter of time before he found them and—

Footsteps sounded in the hall, then the floor shifted slightly under Billy Starrett's weight as he came through the door. "Hey, Taylor, there are two rain slickers downstairs in the kitchen—one of ours and a blue one."

"Mitch and Jennifer," Taylor said grimly. "Search the house. If you find them, shoot them."

Billy didn't protest the way a real cop should but murmured agreement and left the room again. There was a soft whir—the DVD tray retracting—then Taylor walked away from the door. An instant later, the closet door opened and in a mild voice he said, "Hey, Bubba. I am sorry to see you here."

A gasp tried to work its way out, but Jessica muted it with her hand over her mouth. Her legs were trembling, so she huddled in a tighter ball to contain it.

"No sorrier than I am to see you." Mitch's voice was strong, giving no hint of the fear that was about to overwhelm her. He came out of the closet and stopped somewhere near the center of the room.

"What are you doing breaking into my house?"

"The door was already unlocked when I got here."

"It's still unlawful entry. Where is she?"

"Gone. She was going out the back door as you were coming in the front."

"Without her slicker?"

"She was in a bit of a hurry."

"I don't believe you."

Jessica could imagine Mitch shrugging as if he didn't give a damn. "Go ahead and look. You won't find her."

"What are you doing here?"

"Looking for proof."

"Of what?"

"Your involvement in Tiffani Dawn's murder."

There was a moment's surprised silence, then Taylor laughed. "You mean, the bitch left it here? I searched her apartment and her car and her storage unit, and it was here all the freakin' time?"

"Was here. Is gone now."

Jessica had already searched the space where she huddled, but she looked again, this time seeking a weapon. Heavy glasses lined a shelf high above her head, and liquor bottles filled the shelf above that. The only thing she could reach without revealing herself was a package of cocktail napkins, not a prime choice for self-defense.

Moving to her knees, she eased closer to the end of the bar and peeked around cautiously. Mitch faced her, looking implacable, and

Taylor's back was to her. He wore khaki trousers and a polo shirt, both damp from the rain, and his blond hair was glistening with droplets. In his right hand he held a pistol, its barrel aimed at Mitch's chest.

Where was a bottle of twelve-year-old Scotch when you needed it?

As Taylor started to turn his head, she ducked back into her cover. "Hey, Billy! Come in here and see what I found."

Heavy treads sounded in the hall, then Billy came through the door. "Hey, Mitch." He sounded as casual as if he were greeting a friend on the street. "Let me hold that pistol for you." More footsteps, a rustle of movement, then a retreat. "I searched everywhere, Taylor. I didn't find her."

"Mitch says she's gone."

"Oh, yeah?" Billy reached for his radio as Jessica peered once again around the corner. He didn't bother with police speak. "Megan, call all the boys off their storm duties and tell 'em to look for Jennifer Burton. If they find her, bring her in and call me or Taylor."

"Will do, Billy," came the response.

"It wouldn't have come to this if she'd stayed dead the first time you killed her," he murmured to Taylor.

"Yeah, well, the bitch never was very good at doing what she was supposed to," Taylor snapped.

"You won't find her," Mitch said. "She's running for her life." His gaze shifted toward the door, then in Jessica's direction before sliding back to Taylor.

She looked at the door, too. The space between it and the end of the bar was narrow, but she could pass through it. If she made it to the hall without being discovered, she could…escape? Save herself? Leave Mitch to die?

She could distract Taylor and Billy and give Mitch a chance to disarm them. She could find some sort of weapon of her own. She could divide—by running like hell and getting one of them to give chase—and Mitch could conquer.

"Where's the DVD?" Billy asked.

"Jennifer has it," Mitch replied. "She took it and ran."

Billy's next question was directed to Taylor. "You think he's telling the truth?"

"I think it doesn't much matter. They both know about it. They both have to die."

Shivers danced down Jessica's spine and every muscle in her body went taut. She moved into a crouch, wincing at the magnified sounds of clothing rubbing, shoes shifting, lungs gasping. Slowly she straightened, making herself an easy target if either man even glanced peripherally, and she took the first step toward the door. Her legs were unsteady, her nerves atremble, but she forced another step, then another.

"If you kill me, you'll bring more trouble down on your town than you know how to deal with," Mitch said, his tone matching the grim smile he wore.

"You think those half brothers of yours will give a damn that their daddy's bastard is dead?"

"They'll give more than a damn. They'll track you down and kill you—if MBI doesn't get you first." His smile broadened, darkened. "We've got a case on you two, Jimmy Ray and the rest of your boys. We're gonna send you to prison for a long, long time."

"MBI? You're a freakin' MBI agent?"

Jessica took another step, another…and a floorboard creaked. She froze, fear sweeping through her, and darted a look toward Mitch. In an instant he'd gone from brash and threatening to frightened, too. "Run," he said, then planted a side kick square in Billy's chest, knocking him to the floor.

Darting out the door, she raced down the hall, took the back stairs two at a time and rushed across the kitchen. As she jerked the door open, she grabbed her slicker, not for protection from the rain but for the car keys in the pocket, digging them out, dropping the jacket as she ran across the slick deck.

When she left the shelter of the house, the wind hit her with full force, sending her stumbling to the side. The rain was heavy, whipped by the wind, stinging her face and arms, cutting visibility to only a few yards. She ducked her head and ran blindly toward the boat landing.

"Jennifer!" The voice was Taylor's, fueled by pure rage. She risked a look over her shoulder in time to see him leap over the steps from the deck to the yard, barreling toward her.

Terror tightened her chest until she could hardly breathe. Her arms and legs pumped, but the waterlogged grass pulled at her shoes and the lack of oxygen sent spasms through her. If she could make it to the woods, if she could find a place to hide… They were just ahead, just fifty feet. *Go, go,* she chanted silently in her head, and Jen's voice joined in. *Go, go.*

The blow came from behind, a solid tackle that knocked the breath from her body and sent her flying forward. She landed facedown with a grunt of stunned pain, a crushing weight on her back and unbearable burning in her chest. Water surrounded her, and she dragged in a mouthful before breaking the surface, choking and spitting. She was in the creek where Jen had died, where Taylor intended for her to die.

His fingers bit brutally into her arms as he turned her onto her back, still straddling her.

"You should have stayed dead, bitch," he growled. Then, with a look of savage satisfaction, he forced her head under the water again.

She tried to kick, but his knees clamped her legs together. Tried to wriggle away, but his hold was too strong. Frantically she clawed at his hands, his arms, his face, inflicting a gouge painful enough that he momentarily released her with one hand. She struggled to the surface and dragged in a deep, sweet breath. Then, after a jarring slap, he forced her under again, his hands around her throat.

She was going to die just as Jen had died. The realization sapped what little strength she had. Her legs went limp first, followed by her body, her arms, her neck. Darkness was settling in, easing the fear, the sorrow, the longing to be with Mitch just one more time—when Jen screamed her name.

No, Jess! It's not your time! Don't let him win. Don't let him do this.

Tired...so tired. Can't breathe.

Think about Mitch. Come on, Jess, he's special. He risked his life for you. You save yours for him.

Her arms were floating just beneath the surface. Abruptly her right hand jerked to the muddy bottom, barely two feet down, and a hand guided hers to a rock there, closed her fingers around it, helped her bring it out of the water. She held it in both hands, tightened her grip, then brought it down on Taylor's head. The impact vibrated through her arms, but she held on to the rock and hit him again.

His body went rigid. His fingers squeezed tighter for an instant, then loosened, letting her go. Slumping forward, he went under the water with a splash, then surfaced again, facedown, unmoving, until the current swirled around him and carried him away.

Gasping for air, Jessica struggled out of the creek and onto the bank, where she collapsed. Taylor was dead or dying—she knew it with a certainty that she could only guess came from Jen. She'd wanted him to pay for Jen's death with his own life, and now he had. She'd kept her promise.

Every part of her body protested when she stood up. Her face throbbed where Taylor had hit her, and her throat felt scratchy and tight. Every cough brought up creek water, and every step ached as she started across the darkened yards. Back to Taylor's house. Back to Mitch.

She was almost there when an explosion shook the air. The ground rumbled, debris flew and flames burst through the windows of the house. Stopping short, she stared, too horrified to scream, to move, to even cry. Numbness seeped through her. This wasn't happening. Mitch couldn't have been inside the house. She hadn't survived Taylor just to lose Mitch. Fate couldn't be that cruel.

Then, out of the smoke and the flames, a tall, lean figure limped out the back door. He took the steps one at a time, slipping once, catching himself with a low groan. He carried a yellow bundle, cradling it tightly in the crook of his arm, and when he saw her, his pace increased despite the obvious difficulty.

Jessica ran to meet him, throwing herself into his arms, covering his face with kisses. "You're all right! Oh, my God, I thought— You're all right!"

He raised his free hand, knuckles skinned and swollen, to her face, blinking back rain and blood that flowed freely from a gash on his forehead to gaze fiercely at her. "I didn't come here to die, darlin'. I'm the good guy, remember? I defeat the bad guys—and I get the girl, too."

As if to emphasize that, he gave her one of the good kisses, the kind that curled her toes and sent a slow, throbbing heat curling through her belly. It almost made her forget all they'd been through, until she moved closer and he grunted in pain. She stepped back and studied him, noticing the swelling beneath one eye and along his jaw. "Do you look better than the other guy?" she asked hopefully.

Mitch looked from her to the blazing house, and his expression settled into grimness. "Yeah. I do now. He set the fire to destroy any evidence. He didn't expect to get caught in the explosion."

She glanced that way, too. She wasn't sorry— well, maybe a little for Starla. Whatever her flaws, the woman had seemed to adore her husband. But Jessica couldn't summon an ounce of sympathy that he was dead. He'd taken innocent lives. Losing his own life was justice.

Mitch turned his back on the house, slid his arm around her waist and started limping toward the woods. He leaned on her enough that she could feel his weight, a comforting, welcome sensation.

It was an arduous half mile to the Mustang. She eased him into the passenger seat, then ran around and climbed in behind the wheel. After starting the engine, she asked, "Where are we going?"

He grinned, looking pretty beat by the dashboard lights, and held up the bundle—his yellow slicker, she realized. "Jackson. I want to deliver this in person."

"What is it?"

Awkwardly he opened it to reveal a half-dozen DVDs. The top one was Tiffani Dawn's.

Taylor and Billy were dead, but there were others left to punish, Jimmy Ray among them. In a few years, Mitch had said, he figured Jimmy Ray would be in prison or dead. She could live with that.

She backed into the clearing, switched the

wipers to high and started along the gravel lane that led to the street. As the wind slacked and the rain let up, she followed the street into the west side of Belmar, then headed north. Away from town. Away from Jen's nightmare.

And with Mitch.

Epilogue

Taylor's body was found tangled in tree roots along Timmons Creek a quarter mile from his house. The remains of Billy's body were removed from the burned-out house two days after the hurricane blew itself out. Jimmy Ray and a few other officers had been arrested, and a dozen more were under investigation.

And the city of Belmar had offered Mitch a job as the new chief of police.

He'd turned them down.

It was a warm afternoon. The sun was shining, the air was muggy and there wasn't a dark cloud in sight. He and Jessica were headed east along Interstate 20, the top down on the Mustang, the wind blowing through their hair. The speedometer needle hovered around ninety—good for a hefty fine if a state trooper happened to stop them.

Not that she couldn't charm her way out of a ticket. A man would have to be dead to not respond to her.

And Mitch was very much alive. They had proven it multiple times in the past few days.

A sign announcing the upcoming exit for Copper Lake flew past in a blur. "You might want to slow down a little," he advised.

"Hey, you don't own a car like this and not run it once in a while."

"Your name's not on the title yet, sweetheart."

She slowed, changed lanes, then took the exit. At the stop sign, she looked at him. "Are you sure Sara doesn't mind me coming with you?"

"I'm sure."

"You know, she might not like me."

He picked up her hand and studied it. The long pink nails were gone, her own nails unpolished.

She wore shorts a good six inches shorter than her sister's and a tank top that molded to her breasts like a second skin. She looked incredible. Sexy. Beautiful.

She looked like his future.

"I think Sara will like you just fine."

"How do you know that?"

"Because I think I love you, and that's enough to make Sara love you."

Her blue eyes got all soft and hazy for a moment, then she smiled brightly. Pushing the accelerator to the floor, she pulled away from the stop sign with the tires squealing. The wind snatched her words as soon as she spoke them—but not before he heard them.

"I think I love you, too."

* * * * *